Praise for *The Reason for Crows*

"...Glancy does a remarkable job of capturing the voice and thoughts of a girl who has been dead for more than three hundred years and who lived in a time and culture that no longer exist."

— *Magill's Literary Annual 2010*

"In rich and moving images, Glancy creates a girl of questions, confusion, and penance."

— *World Literature Today*

"*The Reason for Crows*, though short, is a complex and deceptively heavy novel. Glancy uses striking imagery in overlapping and contradicting ways to ask engaging and still-relevant questions of her reader. No two people who have witnessed the same event will tell the exact same story, and Glancy handles the different perspectives, tones, and experiences of each narrator very carefully, constructing a version of history that is believable and intelligent."

— *Rain Taxi*

"...a lancingly beautiful journey into pain and spirit."

— *Booklist*

The Reason for Crows

THE
REASON
FOR
CROWS

A STORY OF
KATERI TEKAKWITHA

DIANE
GLANCY

excelsior editions

State University of New York Press
Albany, New York

Published by
State University of New York Press, Albany

© 2009   State University of New York

For information, contact State University of New York Press, Albany, NY
www.sunypress.edu

Production by Marilyn P. Semerad
Marketing by Susan M. Petrie

Library of Congress Cataloging-in-Publication Data

Glancy, Diane.
    The reason for crows : a story of Kateri Tekakwitha / Diane Glancy.
        p. cm.
    Includes bibliographical references.
    ISBN 978-1-4384-2672-3 (pbk. : alk. paper)
1. Tekakwitha, Kateri, 1656–1680—Fiction. 2. Indians of North America—
Fiction. I. Title.
    PS3557.L294R43 2009
    813'.54—dc22

                                                            2008043243

10   9   8   7   6   5   4   3   2

CONTENTS

The blackbird whistling
or just after.

    —Wallace Stevens, *Thirteen*
    Ways of Looking at a Blackbird

Do I have to love a mutant?

    —Leonard Cohen, *Beautiful Losers*

And when I put you out, I will cover the
heaven, and make the stars dark; I will cover
the sun with a cloud, and the moon will not
give her light. I will make the bright lights
of heaven dark over you, and set darkness
upon your land, says the Lord God—

    —Ezekiel 32:7–8

The Indeans have smallpoxe, they fall
downe of diseas, they lye on harde mattes,
their sores break and runn. Their skin
cleaves to their mattes. They are bloodie,
they lye in the cold. Noeone to build a fire
against the snowe or carrye water—

    —Diane Glancy

Many years ago, in New York City, I found an Indian girl on one of the panels of the front doors of St. Patrick's Cathedral. Who was she?—This Kateri Tekakwitha, this Lily of the Mohawks, who lived only twenty-four years.

ACKNOWLEDGMENTS

The cover illustration, *Kateri's Dream: Bird Wing with Claws,* is from a collage workshop by Mary McCleary, March 11, 2006.

Gratefulness to Thirza Defoe for the *Kateri Rock with Smallpox.* The other two rocks are from the trip to Caughnawaga.

I would like to acknowledge the Loft Mentor Series Reading, Minneapolis, Minnesota, for a first reading from the manuscript, April 28, 2006.

Finally, I would like to thank Crystal Alberts for her comments.

CHRONOLOGY

Kateri Tekakwitha:

1656   Born in a Mohawk village, Ossernenon, now Auriesville, N.Y., on the south bank of the Mohawk River.

1676   Baptized at St. Peter's Mission in the Mohawk village Caughnawaga on the north side of the Mohawk River.

1677   Journeyed on the Mohawk River from Caughnawaga through Amsterdam, N.Y., along the Chuctanuda Creek, and an unknown trail to Canada on the south bank of the St. Lawrence at Montreal.

1680   Died at St. Francis Xavier Mission, Kahnawake or Caughnawaga, near Montreal.

The Reason for Crows

KATERI TEKAKWITHA

1656–1680

MOHAWK / ALGONQUIN

KATERI TEKAKWITHA

—Unto thee O Lord I commendeth my soule.

KATERI: The moaning was my first memory. I think it was them—my mother and father. They died in the smallpox epidemic with my infant brother. I was five years old. Black birds gathered waiting for our death. I felt the birds peck my face. In my fever dream, I was floating in a stream. A Spirit lowered its basket to gather water. I was in the water that spilled into the basket. For a while, I was inside God. I floated like a crow.

My mother was Algonquin. My father, a Mohawk chief. I was born in a village called Ossernenon on the south bank of the Mohawk River. My mother was a Christian. My father was not.

The smallpox left its encampment. My parents and brother were gone, though I still had relatives. Children laughed when I passed. Boys turned away from my face. I am not a saint. I am a girl seeking sanctuary. I am scarred. I feel the pits on my face with my fingers. My eyesight is bad—I can look into the woods and see snow that is not

3

there. The shapes of the trees are blurred. This toxic God. This Fire who burns away everything.

I see lions when I sleep. I did not know what a lion was until I saw one in a book in the mission. They have eaten Christians. They are magnificent in their roaring. Jesus is a lion. I often see him with a mane of light.

Smallpox is a crow. Its black wings like the night. Its beak eats my face. If black were an object, it would be water. The way it shapes the rocks in its path.

My name, Tekakwitha, means the one-who-walks-grop-ing-her-way. Or moving-all-things-before-her. It means one-who-puts-things-in-order. Or one-who-bumps-into-things. It is a name that can go several ways. It can have several meanings. But they all have to do with seeing what is before me. Smallpox nearly took my eyesight. I trip my way through the village. Especially in bright light. I see snow— I have said that. But it repeats itself also.

I hardly remember the earth before it blurred.

Is it the same for all who hear the Lord's voice? Mine came with smallpox. The fever of fire. My mother heard the Jesuit's words. She knew the wings. She was given as a wife to a chief who did not believe. She kept her belief. It was a story she carried. A direction she followed. A map she kept through this crow-dark woods.

She taught me faith in Jesus. She belonged to the Maker the Jesuits called God. He sent his son, Jesus, to become a crow on the cross. He became darkness for us. I made crosses with sticks and left them in the woods—tying them at the cross-arms with animal hair or sinew. I tell the rabbits and muskrats about Jesus. Suffering is for a benefit—We come to knowledge of You, O Lord. The animals listen.

My chest is burning. I am nearly blind in the sun. I am pocked.

Lead us through this wilderness of crows. I cry out to you—You are my way. Under your wings I make my refuge until these calamities pass—Psalm 57:1–2. I am drawn to that Psalm. It is a tree standing by itself. It is a copse. It is the voices of the forest shouting.

My mother was an Algonquin Christian of the Weskarini or turtle band. She was taken prisoner by the Mohawk—married to the chief of a tribe different than hers. I do not think she minded being with my father. She seemed happy. But I was young when she died. It might have been different than I knew. My father died in the epidemic with her. Also my brother.

Then my uncle, Iowerano, was chief. I was adopted by his wife, Karitha, and his sister, Aronsen. The women were Christians also.

I was scarred with smallpox, yet I made ribbons from strips of eel skin and painted them red. I tied them in my hair.

I picked corn with my uncle's wife and sister, sometimes holding one hand over my eyes when the light of the sun hurt them. I listened to the forest. The noise of birds as they called to one another. I listened to the wind through the leaves, the water in the rivulets and the river. It was sound I saw.

I carried small bundles of firewood from the forest with the tumpline—the burden strap on my head—I wove the strap with threads from bark strips, threaded and woven together until the stay was strong enough to haul the load of twigs.

I carried water in a small bark bucket. I pounded corn. I could not do the work of other girls and women. I trembled. I sweated. I felt the smallpox again. Or the remains of it. I lay shivering on my mat in the dark of the longhouse until I could get up again.

Anastasia Tegonhatsiongo and Enit stayed with me. They were older *sisters,* friends. Anastasia was a widow. Enit knew she would marry Onas. She talked of him as we worked. I did not think I would ever talk of marriage. I beaded with them, feeling my way with the bone needle and sinew. I remembered the patterns of the beads with my fingers. I felt I could see when I beaded. We had as many beads as the stars.

We made baskets, boxes, buckets, and large bark casks rimmed with hickory splints to store corn, berries, beans.

We treated the wounded when the Machicans attacked our men who were hunting. Often, not many were left alive. We listened to their moans. I think sometimes the spirits suffocated them, helping them leave their wounds in this world. Once, in the dark, I put my hand on something wet and sticky. I felt it again and knew it was hair. It was the scalp of someone dying, not fully severed from his head.

We wove belts to trade for thimbles, glass beads, iron awls, pewter spoons, bells, muskets, lead shots, knives, and nails.

It was the thimbles and glass beads I wanted. The thimbles more than the glass beads.

The smallpox continued. It moved among tribes. We heard of it from a distance. We saw it in our own village. It began with fatigue. Someone could not climb a tree for bird eggs. Then there was nothing they wanted to do. Or could do. Then fever. Headache. Backache. Vomiting. Red spots appeared on the tongue like berries. Then the spots moved to the mouth and throat. The spots turned to blisters. The blisters covered the face. The arms. Legs. Palms of hands. Soles of feet. They were under the eyelids. Joints swelled. There was bleeding. Terrible dreams. Delirium. Pustules crusted over the whole body. Death.

Now I wear a blanket over my head to hide my eyes from the light. But mostly I wear it to cover my pocked face.

I am not able to help those who are sick with smallpox. I am not yet strong enough to turn them on their mats. But I can wipe their sores. Sit beside them. Fan them. The forest holds us in its teeth.

The forest is a lion.

After a few years, the tribe moved upstream, to a hill above the north bank of the Mohawk River to get away from the place of the moaning disease that killed my parents and brother. I hear the forest moan also. I think sometimes it has the disease. I hold the leaves with my fingers. They feel pocked. Maybe the forest suffers what we suffer. Maybe it becomes like us. It is marked like we are marked. It feels what we feel. We are one with it.

I held the hands of Karitha and Aronsen, the wife and sister of my uncle, Iowerano, the chief, as we descended the hill from the old village. They helped me step into the canoe that would take us across the Mohawk River.

We climbed the hill on the other side of the water with our bundles. The sachems blessed the place of the new village. We built longhouses and plant crops. We named the new village Caughnawaga. We marked hiding places in the woods in case of attack.

Sometimes I tremble in the forest. It is the aftermath of the disease. Why do some of us stay on earth, while some of us sit in heaven where the falling stars whiz past?

Sometimes I wake sweating. I wake from the forest dreams when the evil one lurks. I see the trees move where he passes. I hear his roar that lifts through the trees. He is not a lion, but he thinks he is. I often think how the forest is like our Christ. It is stronger than the evil that passes.

I hurt my foot when I tripped over a stump at the edge of the forest. I had a bundle of twigs in my bundle strap. I fell and turned my ankle. My twigs scattered. When I got up, I could not stand. I could not walk. I crawled back to the village. For a long time, I lay on my mat. When I could get up, I limped. I am nearly blind. The light is sharp in my eyes. Sometimes the air swirls before my eyes. I watch it turn over. My face is scarred with smallpox. Yet there is a ribbon of red eel skin in my hair.

There is a commotion outside the longhouse.

I hear the voice of Onas, whom Enit thinks she will marry. He is warning us—Run to the woods. What is happening? I cannot see. I do not know anything until it is upon me. Who is coming? The Machicans? Our enemy tribe? No, this time it is the French soldiers. Often we fear them.

I hear them coming, rattling their guns over the land. I run with others into the woods, Anastasia and Enit now holding my hands, pulling me along because I cannot see the way in my fear. We hide in places the soldiers do not know. We hear shots from their guns. Enit cries out for Onas. Anastasia tells her to be quiet. We hear the crackle of fire. The smell of smoke. I grow dizzy—trees lean over—the sky is slanted. I hear the moan of the flames in our crops. I hear the cries of the corn and beans as they burn.

When Onas calls, Enit runs to him, leaving a hollow place at my side. Maybe the Maker was there, and I just could not feel him. I returned with Anastasia to the village in rubble. The blur I see is the smoke still rising from the ruins of the bark longhouses. The crow wings I see are our burned fields.

The soldiers have destroyed our new village on the north bank of the Mohawk. They have burned all of the crops we planted. The new longhouses we built. Everything is burned. Our woven mats. Our moose-hair and quill work. Our burden straps. Our fish weirs for catching eel. The bow loom to weave wampum belts.

Later, we walk through the ashes. We find the melted glass beads and thimbles. I feel them with my feet. I keep a charred thimble warped from its shape.

Because there are no crops, we are hungry that winter. Anastasia, Enit, and I put on our snowshoes and go into the woods with our digging sticks. We gather roots. We boil bark. We pound acorns mixed with a few dried berries. Once, there was an animal to eat, half dead itself before we killed it. Sometimes there was nothing.

It was in the winter that Enit married Onas Sangorkaskan. My Uncle Iowerano spoke the ceremony. A wooden bench was placed in the center of the longhouse where Enit and Onas sat, each holding their wedding basket they would exchange. I heard my uncle's voice to Enit and her family. What is her name? What clan? Do you accept your daughter's choice? Will you prepare food? Then he directed questions to Onas. Will you provide food? Afterward they exchanged the wampum.

But even when Enit married, we still had little to eat. The hunters returned discouraged. I think it was shame they felt. We had known hunger, but this hunger seemed more severe. We were up against something new. There was a shift in the land. Its voice was troubled. We heard it in the trees. We heard it in the night, the underside of day, when the hunters and night stalkers were out. We used to hear the larger animals that killed the smaller ones. Now it was the cries of the stalked we heard. We felt their fear. The night was embroidered with worms, bugs, burrowers. It was stained with blood. The overside was day. But the trouble of the night stayed with us.

Priests came to the village, but left. Were they the ones that had converted my mother? They sounded like her—they told stories I had heard from her. There was the same feeling—the same spirit. We had seen the traders and trappers. Our dreams were a village where they passed. Now we heard about the settlers. They came from other lands. They came to live where we did. Why had this happened? Why had they left their land and walked across the water in a boat? But did Indian tribes not migrate and drive out other tribes?

Karitha, my uncle's wife, and Aronsen, his sister, grieved.

We will be given to the crows, they said.

They have already taken us with their disease, Anastasia said.

We had not seen this coming. Yes, maybe there had been prophecy, Aronsen remembered. We just did not listen. We were the makers of what came to us—Before the smallpox that was stronger than us. Before the white men came.

They will not leave us alone, Karitha said.

Maybe they will pass around us and leave us as we are, Enit hoped.

No, they would not leave us standing—These settlers with their need to conform us to them—These men who followed us from the overside until they moved in our nightmares.

The old ones had seemed quiet before the smallpox came. Aronsen tried to remember. She was a girl. She did not pay attention. She thought about the warriors. Who she would marry. Who would provide for her. How many children she would have. She thought about her beading. She thought about the bark baskets she was learning to make. She thought about the ribbons in her hair.

I thought about ribbons too. I thought about the feel of beads in my hands. I could feel the patterns with my fingers, though I could not see them clearly. I could feel the thread pulled through the hide. The years were a bark basket we all made. But the years made us bark baskets. We had been filled with something larger than us. We had been overcome. We just did not know it yet. Had the elders seen it and not told us? Had they tried to tell us and we had not listened? Or had we not understood their words?

I felt dark shadows beyond us move. I left the group of women and went farther into the woods to be alone, bumping into trees, feeling my way with a stick. I stayed in the blind trees. What was this horror I felt?—This horror I could almost see. The Maker would protect us from whatever would happen. He would not allow anything else to come. I remembered the smallpox epidemic I lived through. I was hauled into death, but pulled back out. I do not know why. Maybe I was set apart for the Lord. No one else would have me.

Was it the darkness beyond the grave I felt? Was it the darkness of the sachem's words I could give up for the assurance of God?

We planted new fields and rebuilt on the sand flats, and named the new village Caughnawaga after the old village. We placed cut tree trunks upright in a wide circle and built our longhouses inside the walls.

I fell over a log as I tried to help. Afterward, my foot throbbed. For several days, I hobbled with a stick. For several more days I lay on my mat in the new longhouse that smelled of the forest. But soon the air was greenish, underwater-like, from the smoke of new cooking fires.

Do you want to ride to the border with me? It was a voice I was sure I heard. What was it? This forest moan. This garish haze. Our longhouses and the walls of our village had once been trees. Now they were broken. But I had broken apart also. I could comfort the forest voices that also had been broken to make our village. I am water. I cannot tell you how. Little feathers are falling. There are whirls of air.

The Jesuits arrived at Caughnawaga, our village, after a treaty with the French colonial government. My uncle tolerated them. They did not carry guns. I had seen them pass through our village; now they stayed here.

I looked at the priests. Their blurred images were like dark spots before me. Who were these black figures who had preached their religion to my mother and aunts? These men dressed as crows without wings. No, they have wings. They unfold from the Book they carry. They were the ones my mother had talked about.

I was afraid, then I was not afraid. Fathers Fremin, Bruyas, and Pierron built a bark church and named it St. Peter's Mission. For days, I heard the pounding and the noise. I saw the little point of the cross they placed on the roof above the door. I saw the strike of sun on—what was it? Metal, Onas said.

What is that clang?

A bell, Anastasia said. That is what they call it.

The bark church was small and drafty. Whenever I was there, I thought of a fish-trap poorly made.

Now there was commotion again. The women cried out in terror. I tripped over a rolled mat and was nearly trampled. We thought the French soldiers were back. Onas was gone in an instant. Our warriors went after—who was there this time?

The Machicans, Enit said. I could hardly hear her above the noise. It was our enemy tribe. They had sneaked up, trying to attack before we knew they were there. But our warriors sprang after them, wanting to protect the new crops and village. They went after them with revenge they would have placed on the French soldiers.

When the warriors returned, they brought the Machican captives to torture. I would not watch them, though they were Machicans who attacked and tortured us. Sometimes the Machicans died without crying out. Other times they went crazy with pain. Sometimes I was relieved I did not have clear sight. I had seen smallpox. I had seen the Torturer. That was enough.

FATHER PIERRON: St. Peter's Mission, Caughnawaga, in the New World. I witnessed the torture of Machican captives. I cannot bring myself to write about the particulars. But I can say the Mohawks torture their captives to the point of death, but stop short of it. They want their captives alive to torture in the same way the next day and the next. They work to prolong the torture.

I sat with the captives at night. The Mohawks did not stop me. I nursed the wounded. I wrapped their wounds. I prayed for them. I sang a Gregorian chant for them. They asked me to continue singing. The pain seemed to lessen. Or their moaning did at any rate. I told them about God. I offered them heaven. They accepted my prayers. God received them into his kingdom through Christ. I prayed for the Mohawks, even when I gagged on my prayers.

KATERI: I was on my mat in the longhouse when one of the crows entered. He was a new priest—Father James de

Lamberville, he said, who had joined the others. I do not think he expected to find anyone. I think he was curious about our houses. Everyone else was in the fields. He looked in and found me. He started telling me about Christ. My mother had been a Christian, but my father, who was dead, and my uncle, who was now chief, were not. He was difficult to understand, but sometimes he talked with his hands, and I knew what he was saying. I told him I would like to be baptized as my mother had been, but I knew my uncle did not want it. Father de Lamberville asked me to start coming to St. Peter's chapel to pray with him.

At first, I came and went to the church of St. Peter's for prayer. Who noticed me with smallpox on my face? Usually everyone turned away. I hid my visits from my uncle. My aunts had been baptized. When they knew where I was, they made no objection.

I listened to the Book Father de Lamberville read because of the animals—the squirrels that made their nests in trees. The desert owl. The vulture, cormorant, eagle, moose, deer, rabbit, caribou, ox, gazelle, roe, locust, leech, fish, beaver, muskrat, mosquito, gnat.

Where is the porcupine who gives us our quills for sewing? I ask. And what is a camel?

He is like a lion—but his legs are taller, his face narrower. He has a hump on his back. He does not eat flesh.

I make these little birds of reference.

I knew them in the wilderness and in the land of drought. I am like a lion; like a leopard by the way. I will meet them like a bear that is bereaved of her cubs. I will tear the fat of their hearts and will devour them like a lion— Hosea 13:5–8.

I knew the animals, but what was drought? How would I know it when the woods dripped with rain? When I lived by a river? I saw the Fathers tripping over themselves to read to us. I saw they did not know what we did not know. How could we understand the place that gave the scriptures with its world across the sea? I heard Anastasia and Enit ask, Why did they make it so fearful?

It had been downhill since the other men came from their lands, the blackrobes clattering with them. Smallpox was not the only disease. The spotted leopard the priest read about had other children. It was not his fault. He did not know he brought disease. It came with him silently. Invisibly. Like the wind. Like spirits in the forest. Like beasts that took our children. Like wind. As for the priests—it was their mission, their work, their vision. How long has it been since your last confession?

I waited for the priest to read again. A multitude of camels will cover you—Isaiah 60:6. I waited for him to read about the trees. I will set in the desert the fir tree, and the pine, and the box tree together—Isaiah 41:19. The Lord God wrote the trees of the forest into his words. His writing was like beading. I felt the red berries, the gnarls of roots like scalps.

I know the trees of the forest. I hear their voices when I walk. I know the forest floor. The pine-needle covering. The net of webs and nests in trees. The thick boughs over me. I think sometimes God is a tree. He is many trees. He hides the animals. He speaks to me. I think it is God. HE is a mystery. HE is the only thing I want. I feel drawn to HIM more all the time. My unworthiness is ever before me. I fall on my knees before HIM. I want to beat myself because of my unworthiness.

Birds spring from the grasses when I walk in the field. I find a matted place where a rabbit had nested. Overhead, I hear the scorn of a crow.

The priests continued to read scripture. At first, my hearing has smallpox. I hear only about the animals and trees. The bulls and goats. The badger and ants. Every beast of the forest is mine. I know the fowls of the mountains and the wild beasts of the field—Psalm 50:10–11.

The trees sang their song. They wrapped their branches around me. I became a bough of leaves on their trunk. I sang like the trees sang. *Ahhhhhssss. Ahhhhhssss.* Like that. They sounded like the river where the water is rapid. *Ahhhhhssss. Ahhhhhssss.* They sounded like that—

I cannot see the particulars of the leaves, but the overall blaze of yellow leaves when they turn before winter. Then I see the gnarl of bare trees barely visible without their leaves. I can hear the rustling of the women walking to the fields. The hunters returning from the woods.

The Machicans came near our village again. They killed several of our hunters and scalped a woman. I held her head on my lap until she died. Father Bruyas sprinkled her forehead with his holy water. She passed into the next world with the red sun going down through the trees.

Afterward, I washed my sticky hands and dress in the river.

In the long, harsh, blessed winters, Fathers Fremin, Pierron, Bruyas, and de Lamberville read to us. Often Fremin and Pierron traveled to other villages and settlements.

He destroyed the sycamores with frost—Psalm 78:47. But it was only the leaves that had fallen from the trees in our forest.

In the snow, Anastasia, Enit, and I walked into the woods in our snowshoes, shawls, and burden straps. We gathered our fagots, our bundles of twigs for fuel.

I thought of Kisisok?e, the sun woman in my mother's Algonquin tribe. I would have prayed to her in the cold, but my mother would have told me to put those old beliefs away.

My feet walk among the stumps of oak when they are felled—Isaiah 6:13. I am like a green fir tree—Hosea 14:8.

These scriptures are falling stars. They come in sheets of light. Red wings of flames fling inward to the dark. His bread is thrown to us, crumbling in the Milky Way.

When Father James de Lamberville came into the long-house, I had told him I wanted to be baptized. I knew my uncle was against the Christians. Often he spoke against them. Often Iowerano was mad at his wife and sister because of their prayers. I wanted to please my uncle, though I knew my mother was a Christian also. She had been baptized by missionaries. She told me about going into the water. I was five when she died. How could I remember her story? How did she tell me in a way I remembered? It was when she bathed me—I remember she said there was a holy bath—I felt her hands on my head. They felt like water. I think it was my first memory. How many times did she tell me before I remembered?

memories, emotions w/ phys. connection

I took religious instruction from the Jesuits. Sometimes they themselves were sick, but not with smallpox. I learned about Matins. Vespers. Their masses. Their liturgies. Their smells. Their prayers. Their cawings. I saw their cross with Christ upon it, pocked with holes from thorns in his forehead, pocked with holes from nails in his hands and feet. He had known smallpox. I listened to the priests read scriptures. I always waited for the passages about the animals and the trees. Especially the trees. It was what I heard in the forest.

This silence. This excitement.

There was no writing in Mohawk. I could not read English. I did not know French. But Father de Lamberville knew enough Algonquin that I could understand what he said, maybe some of what he said.

It was a voice I had known anyway.

It was more than language sometimes. It was light. In God's light I saw light. Some of the priest's words I also came to know.

These are Notes he keeps under his crow wings. The Priest's Journey—he calls them. That is why the sleeves on his robe are shiny, even more so in the rain and snow. That is why the light rubs off from them. That is why my fingers shine. I have touched his sleeves. I follow his path of writing.

FATHER JAMES DE LAMBERVILLE: In the Year of our Lord 1674, at the Mohawk village of Caughnawaga in the New World—I walked into one of their lodges—a dark longhouse. The air burned my eyes. It was filled with the smoke of their cooking fires. How did they breathe? I thought the longhouse would be empty. Everyone was in the fields. But there was a girl on a mat in a state of weakness. As I neared, I saw the mound of her face—small, brown, and pox-bitten. I drew back from the sight of her. When I recovered myself, I talked to her about coming to church.

I sat in the bark church thinking how to speak to them—the Indians like stories. They are used to listening. I would read the Bible as if telling a story. The Jesuits read to us in the refectory when I was a student. I liked the readings. With the pock-marked girl, I read scripture about the animals and trees. I knew the forest was important to them. I tried to reach them by what they understood.

I eat this book—Ezekiel 3:1. I memorize. As they walk, I wind a rope around their feet to remind them we all are bound to the Lord. I try to teach them how they trip up themselves in the face of the Lord when they follow their own ways. The girl trips anyway. Her name means she-who-walks-searching-in-front-of-her. She does not always see what is there. How do I tell the Indians my visions? I was in my house when I saw a hand stretched toward me. In it was a scroll—Ezekiel 2:9.

If you say to the wicked, you shall surely die, and you give him no warning, to save his life, that same wicked man will die in his iniquity; but his blood will be on your hands. If you warn the wicked, and he does not turn from his wickedness, he will die in his iniquity, but you have delivered your soul—Ezekiel 3:18–19.

It is my job to tell them. It is my job to convert the heathen. I have been sent to the Indians—impudent, rebellious, stiff hearted. Those are the prophet Ezekiel's words in the Old Testament.

In eight months at St. Peter's Mission, I baptized only fifty-three—

Postscript to Father de Lamberville, by FATHER PIERRON: Yes, infants and dying children. Sick ones out of their head. The Machicans they captured were tortured. I slap my hands together. My fingers are eaten with cold. My hands squeak like birds. My fingers crack as bird claws. In the cold, the cracks bleed. Is this my stigmata?

FR. P.: STAY OUT OF MY NOTES—FR. L.

FATHER JAMES DE LAMBERVILLE: Often the others were gone. Father Fremin to the Iroquois. Father Bruyas to the Oneida. Father de Lamberville in the scriptures with Ezekiel. There were upsets, one after another. Disease. The whiskey the Dutch traders brought. The wars between the Mohawks and Machicans.

Provisions are scarce and difficult—small game, some meal for a few cakes, dried berries—most of them the Indians give to us though they are hungry themselves.

We lost as many as we converted. They returned to their Indian ways and did not come to church. They hold dreamfests. They play *dream guessing*. They commerce with dark spirits of the Mohawk gods. They like the evil one. They are rowdy. Corporeal. They do not follow rules: prayer twice a day and church attendance.

I have seen the burnings, the torture, and the scourgings of their enemies. They dance their dance with crows.

They worship hills, ravines, valleys, rivers, animals, trees.

Christian Indians would not attend these rituals because of their Christianity. We have caused division in their tribe. The blessed division of the wheat from the tares. The sheep from the goats.

I am eating scrolls. I have my mouth full of them.

FATHERS FREMIN, BRUYAS, PIERRON: St. Peter's Mission, the New World. I hide my words among others in order that I do not take pride in these words I write—these likenesses I make with my writing.

We read the *Spiritual Exercises* of St. Ignatius:

Represent to yourself the flames of hell, and in the midst of the flames an innumerable multitude of fallen angels.

With prayer and supplication we come before you, O Lord, our Magnificent One. We pray for the souls of these heathen. We come before you O Lord of Hosts to intercede for the lost. We have given up our country, our comforts, for these. Have mercy, O Lord. Spare them the flames of hell.

Represent to yourself Adam driven from Paradise by an angel armed with a fiery sword and not knowing where to hide his shame and remorse.

We come to you O God in the Magnificence of Your Being. You are our comforter, the restorer of what has been lost. You are the One who measured the cost. We follow You. We walk in Your Way. May we receive cover for our sins from You. In Your Blood we are washed. By Your Spirit we are renewed. We hide our shame and remorse in You.

KATERI: How do I understand the Fathers? They speak a few words I understand. I am learning more. When I hear their voices lifted in chapel, I fly with them. It is the rhythm of their words. It connects with something I know. The Jesuits' stories are about God, the Maker, the Old One, who is in my spirit opening the way for his words.

FATHER JAMES DE LAMBERVILLE: The hand of the Lord was heavy on me. I sat in the bark church and prayed.

I, who have seen the cathedrals in France. I, who have sat in them. I, who have spoken from their altars. I, who have felt their holy fortresses. I have touched the light that came through the windows. I, who have tasted the pastries of France. The stews. The oysters. The sauce au beurre.

FATHER P: Poisson. Poulet. Canard. Pommes de terre. Artichauts. Aubergines. Sauce à la moutarde. Sauce crème.

FATHER JAMES DE LAMBERVILLE: None of the Indians came. I gave my sermon before the empty room. The walls listened. The pews. The plank floor. The next day I opened my windows. I preached. The grass heard. The rabbits. The sky. The skies. How many of them over us? How many layers up there?

Take a clay tablet, build a siege wall against it, heap up a mound against it like those mounds the Indians scrape together to plant their corn—Ezekiel 4:1. I pasted my prayers on the sides of the church house. Still the Indians did not come.

I saw what no one in a cathedral saw. These pitiful people across the sea, full of scabs and scars and ignorance. The deceiver has them in his hands.

The pocked girl came often to the church. One morning she brought three children with her. I invited them in. Of such is the kingdom of God. Thus, my congregation. My flock. Eventually, other women came with them. I tell them I am captivated by Ezekiel. His resolve gives me strength. Shut yourself up in your house—Ezekiel 3:24. I read several passages. They cannot understand my language—it is Latin I choose from time to time—but the light of language captivates them. Sometimes I see their eyes float above me as I speak. I trust the Lord is sending them visions to authenticate what I say.

Ezekiel shaved his head with a knife and burned his hair before the people who would not believe—Ezekiel 5:1. Should I consider the same?

None of my words kept them in church, except for this strange-looking, pock-marked girl who survived the smallpox epidemic the Dutch traders brought—Tekakwitha. My tongue trips over her name as she trips over benches in the church she cannot see. Some of her friends and relatives wander in and out also. I cannot always tell. One of them has a husband, Onas, who seems interested in the gospel.

I ask to marry them in the Christian tradition. They agree. How good it is to have Onas to talk to about the Iroquois confederation. How good it is to learn about the savages from him. He seems at times not one of them.

I continue reading scripture, trying to reconcile, to understand direction. They will fall by pestilence, sword, famine—Ezekiel 6:11. Have they not fallen already from smallpox and the Machicans?

Yet I keep reading Ezekiel. I felt I could understand the visions of the Old Testament prophets now that I was in the Indian village. This place so near the gates of hell—I could feel the breath of the evil one. I could hear the flames. My flesh crawled. It was more than the lice. It was the evil one who was used to holding the Indians between his teeth. If only I could snatch them to Paradise. God keeps his doors closed to fool us. I could believe hell was ice in this climate. I have chilblains, chills, frostbite, and shiverings in this ice-house of America.

I sat in my house when I saw a man who looked like a fire and a brightness. His hand lifted me by my hair between earth and heaven—Ezekiel 8:2–3.

I snuck into their longhouses. I saw the drawings on their walls—creeping things and abominations of their own making that did not please God—Ezekiel 8:10. Therefore, I will act in my fury. I will not have pity. When they cry, I will not hear—Ezekiel 8:18.

The evil one still keeps them in darkness. Some of them anyway.

The scribe came with his inkhorn. Go through the city and put a mark on the foreheads of the men who sigh and cry over the wrongdoing—Ezekiel 9:4. Lord, I ask for that mark. Forgive them.

Help me overcome discomfort. Help me not to look back.

KATERI: I am ugly. I am ugly. I hate everyone not pocked. The priests' faces chap in the cold. They grow beards. They grow hair to hide their face. I could tell the weather by the way they walked, hunched, cloaked, as if I did not know weather I could tell by watching them. The trees watch.

They, who have stood a long time. They laugh. The priests do not know. They think theirs is the only way. They do not know the trees do not like them. Those priests tripping over themselves in the bark church. The sky is pocked with stars. I am not alone. The Lord walks with the sky and the earth. Which of his sleeves do I see? Which of his squawks do I hear?

What is this I feel? What is calling me? Who is it? How did it happen to me, and not others? Why did I hear when others did not? Only Anastasia, Enit, her husband, Onas, and a few others. My uncle's wife, Karitha, and his sister, Aronsen, were Christians, but they did not hear Christ the way I did. They did not question. Who was this man who asked for everything and gave nothing in return but promise for eternal life? How can I explain to my uncle? I feel a pull. A certainty. I feel doubt. Anger. I feel a questioning of what I felt. I have nothing certain, but a belief that God is.

If you confess with your mouth the Lord Jesus, and believe in your heart God raised him from the dead, you will be saved—Romans 10:9. How could my Uncle Iowerno understand that? Why would he want to?

When I was old enough to marry, my family tried to arrange a marriage for me.

NO!! I refused. They did not understand. They insisted. I needed a husband who would hunt, who would fight the French—the Machicans. Who would secure the village. Give strength to the tribe. Bring meat to the family. But the boys pointed to me. I saw their arm outstretched when I passed. No warrior would want me. He would grow tired of the crow marks on my face. I would be mistreated because of my ugliness. I could not carry burdens. My leg would not bear weight. But it was more than that. I did not want to marry. I wanted to study with the priest.

Once, coming into the longhouse, I saw a man sitting with my Uncle Iowerano, his wife, Karitha, and his sister, Aronsen. My uncle told me to sit down by him. They asked me to offer him sagamire to eat. This meant I would promise to marry him. I did not want a husband. I ran from the longhouse and hid in the fields. When it was dark, I moved to the corn bin, away from the woods. I did not come near the longhouse until I heard them call that they would not make me marry.

Even my friends, Anastasia and Enit, argued that I needed to marry—Who would provide for me? They asked. Anastasia was a widow, but Enit had married.

How could I marry when I heard the prophets' visions? How could I marry when I wanted the visions myself? I wanted to study with the crows. Then what did my puberty rights mean?—if not time to take a husband?

What would happen to our people? Anastasia asked—She meant those who did not believe what the priests said. How would they get to the sky? How would they make the journey to the Maker?—The Ancient One the priests talk about.

Who wants to go there? My Uncle Iowerano asked.

I do. I said. I do.

I remembered when the Jesuit entered the longhouse with his crow wings folded. His beak guideth me.

There were times the dark spirits rubbed against me. Get away, Father de Lamberville taught me to say—There is nothing of you in me. There were times Christ flew down to me. I saw the trail of his flames.

Father James de Lamberville read the scriptures for scriptures to read to us. He told us about the cherubim in Ezekiel—they had four faces, a man, a lion, an ox, an eagle. They had hoofed feet on wheels and wings. They were full of eyes.

There were animals in heaven, they said.

The Indian spirits were counterfeit of these.

If I confess with my mouth, I belong to the Lord Jesus Christ. Something happens inside me. I am different than I was. I am set apart for God. Am I the only one? No, there is Anastasia, Enit, Onas, and others at Caughnawaga. No, the priest said there are many more Indians in the Christian village farther north. I could go live with them until God calls me from this earth.

May it be soon. May it be soon.

I want to see what this is all about. I want to see faith become substance as it is promised in the word. God asks us to take a risk. He asks us to give all.

I am not worthy. I am not worthy. How can I make

myself worthy? How can I make God not sorry he sent his son to die for us? How can I show God I believe? How can I help my village?

The priest hears my confession.

How can I be worthy? I repeated. I cannot. I cannot. How can I separate from all that I am, to follow him? Why did he speak to me? How can I know it is him?—The God of mercy. Did he see me more pitiful than others? Did he show me his mercy because I was battered with disease? How did it happen that I would hear? I was weaker and without resistance?

I was unfaithful to both Algonquin and Mohawk. *Behold the traitor comes. Stand out of her way before she trips and falls on you.*

Father de Lamberville lifted me to my feet as I agonized in the bark church at St. Peter's Mission. He told me I was ready for baptism.

Several weeks passed before I was baptized in St. Peter's chapel with the water from the spring down the hill outside our village. My uncle did not come to the ceremony, though Karitha and Aronsen did. They sat with Anastasia and Enit and others who were Christians. I was given the name Kateri, or Katherine in English. I was Kaia'tano:ron. Kateri Tekakwitha.

When Father de Lamberville touched my head with water, it was as if I was in the water. I was the water. I remembered my mother's hands on my head when she bathed me. I remembered when I was sick with smallpox, being in the water, floating away, then I was in a basket. A Spirit held me there. It was as if it were something that had already happened.

I held my hands over my eyes.

What do you see? The priest asked.

The Lord on his wheels, I answered.

Father de Lamberville gave me a rosary. The little beads were wheels. My fingers rolled over them, the way the soldiers' cannons rolled over the land, full of awe and fear. I had the feeling I was going somewhere. Something was happening when I prayed. They were medicine beads. Wampum beads. They were cherubim wheels. They were wheels within wheels. Everything was carried on wheels.

The priests talked of St. Francis Xavier Mission on the Sault St. Louis in Quebec. It was a haven for Indian Christians. Enit and Onas, her husband, were planning to go. They persuaded Anastasia to go with them.

After I was baptized, I would not work on Sunday because scripture forbid it. The Sabbath was for rest. Then my family decided I would not eat on Sundays. They took my rosary. Others threw stones. I could not see them before they hit. I could not hold my hand up against them. Sorcerers scorned me. A young man rushed into the longhouse as if to strike me with his tomahawk. I stood before him, unflinching. He left.

There were troubles branching over me. My uncle's wife, Karitha, heard me in prayer. *My Father. My Father.* She thought I was talking about Iowerano. I had to argue with her that I was praying to God, my Father, and not her husband, who was my uncle.

I thought more of the refuge at Sault St. Louis for Christian Indians. Fathers Fremin and Pierron already had gone also. Anastasia and Enit and her husband were leaving. Would I come with them?

But how could I leave? How could I choose between the French Jesuits or the traditional Mohawk ways I had always known?

The Jesuits' rules were not difficult: go to prayer twice a day, go to church every Sunday, do not go to Onnon-houarori, the dreamfests, that were filled with *savage rowdiness,* as the priests called it. But it was spirits from another world they did not know, and would be terrified of if they did, that came over us like a headdress and moved us to their will.

There were encumbrances the tribe felt every day. There were difficulties. In the dreamfest, we felt them go away. In the revelry, the hardships were forgotten. I felt the arousal to dance—even to think about it. I wanted to run to the priests to escape Onnonhouarori.

My Uncle Iowerano said he would smash my head with a hatchet if I tried to leave, but I knew he would not.

I sat alone when they left—Enit, Onas Sangorkaskan, and Anastasia—until the trees came and held my hands.

FATHER JAMES DE LAMBERVILLE: I saw Katherine Tekakwitha's torment. The Indians would not leave her alone. She was a traitor to their ways.

I was acquainted with apostasy. There were many Indians who declared Christianity then returned to old ways. The most despicable was a monthlong drunken dreamfest. Masked revelers ran through the village bringing turmoil. It was a tribal madness—visceral, indecent, violent.

I read Ezekiel 32:8. It was as if God had set darkness on their land.

I wrote Father Chauchetière who had come to Sault St. Louis from France. I told him to receive Anastasia, Enit, and her husband. I told him about Katherine Tekakwitha and my hopes that she would join them. Fathers Fremin and Pierron had moved to Sault St. Louis. Father Bruyas often was gone. I remained to stand with the cross at St. Peter's Mission.

They are tormented by the diseases we brought.

Forgive us, Lord.

They are at it for nights. I hear its rhythms. I pick up the sensual revelry. Do you know what they are without God? Look at the Onnonhouarori. The dreamfest is they way they think they taste God. But they have smallpox sores in their mouth. Red and festering. My mouth is dull as a wafer. It flies away to heaven. I know ambiguity. I know what I do not allow myself to feel. I have chosen this sparseness. But just beyond my sacrifice is the fullness of the Godhead. I know it, not by sight, but faith.

I am shaping Katherine Tekakwitha in spite of the noise in the village. I help her look into the book she cannot read. The sparseness—The sparseness, I say. Then she leaves for the night. I cannot leave her unprotected. Come back. You cannot go on your own. I cannot give her up. I do not want her to be tempted with the dreamfest. I want to hold the edge of her skirt to my neck. I want to break out of these robes. Their weight on my shoulders. So this is what sends them to one another—Man and woman. I could join the revelry—Fall into it—Make this first little step—But then I would be into it. This is what makes men fall—This feeling that grips my loins.

I long for the drunkenness of passion—

I open scripture for a weapon against this feeling. He brought me to the door of the court; and when I looked, behold, a hole in the wall. Then he said to me, Son of man, dig now in the wall; and when I had digged in the wall, behold a door. And he said to me, Go in, and behold the wicked abominations that they do there—Ezekiel 8:7–9.

I fell on my knees in a vision. All was darkness and in the darkness a wall. I dug into the wall and there was a room lit with fire—filled with dancing ones dancing all sorts of frenetic movements. There it was—the untempered heart of man. The burning room of man's desires—his furnace room. Do you know what *we* are without God?

I thought of the furnace in which Shadrach, Meshach, and Abednego were placed. It was a holy fire they withstood. But this vision I saw was a dance with the devil. I pulled back. I looked away. I cried for the spirit of evil that came upon them—Upon all the people of the land that did not have scripture. I felt the edges of it—even in the church of St. Peter's Mission at Caughnawaga. It was a beast of fire. It could even enter the bark walls of the church. I cried for us all—We would die in this fire-death. Save us, O God. I pleaded for the souls of the people. I pleaded for my own soul. I fought my own fire. I fought for my priesthood—I cried out to God that I would not forsake my vow of celibacy. I stood up and took the sword that was the word of God and beat against the flames. I beat and beat until I fell on the floor again.

Where there is no vision, the people perish—Proverbs 29:18. I yelled out the scripture. I felt the words of scripture in my mouth. I felt the transubstantiation of the spoken word in my mouth. It became bread. I chewed it. I tasted the word of God. I swallowed the scripture.

I was divided between my will and my will. My will divided into something I wanted to do, and something I did not want to do. The one I did not want to do was not as strong as the one I wanted to do. I could not stop this feeling. What could I do? I could feel it, but not give into it, not even by my own hand. If I gave in once—even once, I would be lost. I had to send Katherine away to the new Caughnawaga with my involuntary will that was the size of a boulder, and my voluntary will that was the size of a berry. It would be like the pebble David threw at Goliath. I held to the doorpost of the church. How long does this last?—How long until the giant falls after I have thrown this pebble?

KATERI: I believe the birds carry messages for us. I find a feather. I hear the praises of the birds. I find one dead on the ground. I feel the hole in its wing. The birds act out scriptures, crucifying themselves.

I understand the Christ on the cross. He took our darkness upon himself. Yes, we had known darkness, but then God showed his light. I saw it. I held it as my own. Would that it moved with me as I moved—yet it did.

I felt the daily death and resurrection of the sun. The changing shape of the moon. The visitation of the fish in the river. They say, *he is, he is, he is. He has made us.* Then abruptly I hear the priest's cawing.

I wake in the morning with the mystery of a dream—I give birth to birds—

FATHER JAMES DE LAMBERVILLE: A new winter is upon us early. Are we not glad? How sound carries in this frigid air. How I am taken with paroxysms of cold. Frigid shiverings I can hardly control. I am haunted by the Indians' belief in ghosts. I think I see them sometimes myself. When I step outside the mission, I feel the inhabitation of their sorcerers—all things against scripture. I would pour words into their ears if God's word was something I could hold in my hand. But it is. If only they understood transubstantiation. If only I understood.

FATHER _____: How does anyone survive? I denied the body. I lived with penance. I did my chores. I washed in cold water. I ate a meager meal. I ate meagerly. Meagerly.

My hands were cold. The fingers did not want to bend. I looked at them swollen and reddened as if something other than what they were. I look at them as strangers.

What a coarse God to give us this cold.

I lay meagerly on my bed. I heard a brother chop wood for a meager fire.

I hear meagerness in the woods. I am silent in my cell. A brother comes with broth to put in my mouth. I say morning prayers. It is evening, the brother says. I say my evening prayers.

KATERI: I am from here, I tell myself in Algonquin. Nindond?je anic dac nindend?je. Yet I am called to a different place. I feel the moving before it is time. Ketsa:nis. I am scared, I say in Mohawk. I go into the woods, feeling my way between the trees. I speak to the animals:

w?w?ck?chi	deer
m?nz	moose
w?boz	rabbit
nikik	otter
amik	beaver
makwa	bear
k?k?k?h?	owl
mikin?k	turtle
w?gosh	fox

I call the animals by both their names. The priests have names for the animals. And the Dutch. And the Machicans.

How many names do they have? What is this language divided between different sounds? It is not separate words, but a combination, a tribe of sounds that moves through the trees, hissing, roaring, as it fishes for meaning, for contact with another for understanding.

I hear the priests sing. I take off my moccasins. I pile snow on my bare feet. It is soft as beaver pelt. What is this dividing rod? This staff of light that comes through the darkness? Why am I drawn when it reviles nearly everyone else? The Dutch and French traders. The Indians who believe in water panthers and thunderers. Who believe in evil spirits but no hell. *No hell!!* Iowerano stomped his hands on the ground.

Does God pull only certain ones toward him, leaving others for hell? The Mohawk and Algonquin do not believe in hell. Is it, then, not there for them, if they do not believe it is? But for the Christians, who believe it is there, it is there for them? But Christians believe in Christ, therefore, they are saved from hell. So who is hell for? What is hell? The torment of burning villages by the French soldiers? Small pox is a burning from hell. Hell is separation from God, the priests say. It is a place where there always is the smell of burning longhouses. My feet felt the fire of hell. They throbbed in the snow. Yes, the hell the priests warn against was there.

I did not stop hearing about the mission where Christian Indians lived. Anastasia, Enit, and her husband were there. They sent messages for me to come. I knew how to be alone inside my darkness. I knew how not to trust the blurred images I saw.

Was I only fleeing the sorcerers? The sachem's words? My uncle Iowerano's tobacco blessing? The ceremonies for seed planting, bean harvest, new corn, and corn harvest were the hardest to ignore. It was the simple ones that nested in my thoughts.

Was I only fleeing the criticism? The mockery? The rocks thrown at me by boys? The horrid dreams that crawled like snakes through my sleep? The fear of hell?

Here it came again. I walked through the field from the spring. I heard a group of boys. When I passed them, a rock hit my head. I half expected it, but this rock was harder. I fell forward in the field spilling the basket of water.

I had given up hope of leaving. But one day a man came from the northern mission. His Oneida name was Hot Ashes because he had been known for his temper before his conversion. Now he spoke with the Mohawks. He said Christianity had power over the diseases we suffered from the Dutch. It was stronger than the liquor from the French. His English name was Louis Guronhiague. His French name, Poudre Chaude. He came with Enit's husband, Onas, and Jacque, a Huron. They hid the canoe by the edge of the lake. They prompted me to come with them back to the mission. It was me they had come for and anyone else who would come. I had gone to St. Peter's chapel. I talked with Father de Lamberville. He said, *go*. I had his blessing. I had my dream of the birth of birds.

When I heard Hot Ashes speak, I knew I would go to the St. Francis Xavier Mission.

My uncle Iowerano was visiting with the Dutch about further trade. He was gone from the village.

That night, in the dark, I got up and stepped away from Karitha and Aronsen. I went to the river.

I sat in the canoe waiting the return of Hot Ashes, who still was trying to persuade other Indians to come with him. But no one else came. I waited with the two men by the river until Hot Ashes came.

That night, I fled St. Peter's Mission in the village of Caughnawaga. I would move to Sault St. Louis, St. Francis Xavier Mission near Montreal, to a village with the name of Caughnawaga. From Caughnawaga to Caughnawaga.

I left Caughnawaga by the rapids of the Mohawk River. I went to Caughnawaga by the St. Lawrence.

The three men paddled. I felt the movement of the canoe over the water of the Mohawk River. Slipping over the water, I was walking on air. I carried one possession—the burnt thimble from the fire at the old village at Caughnawaga. I let it fall into the water.

As we wooded that night, someone came after us. The men hid me under blankets. Whoever it was passed us in the woods as if we were invisible. Had it been Iowerano? Was it a spirit?—The evil one? I did not know. Could I *be* outside my village? I wanted its walls around me. I wanted to be in the longhouse. I wanted our mats and storage baskets around me. What was this travel into a new land? This crossing. Was I anything more than a filament? The darkness was large. It reached to the sky. It filled the sky. The evil one scouted his territory. I heard his steps. I felt his breath on my neck. I felt the evil one pulling me up. I could go back. The evil one would lead me. No—Anastasia and Enit were ahead. I would be with them in a new village. I thought of my parents in the sky above me—my mother trying to sweep away the darkness. I felt I was suspended off the ground. There seemed to be an orange light around me as if the fire pit in the longhouse. Was I back? No, it was not a cooking fire. I put my hands to my mouth to hold back the fear. I would resist the power I felt. I had chosen this trip. I would go. I had committed myself to Christ. Nothing else had power over me. I pushed the evil one away, and he departed.

We followed the Chuctanuda Creek. Northward. Always north. Sometimes the men portaged the canoe. When they hunted, I stayed with the canoe. I walked on the edge of the woods. I saw something. A tree stump? A black bear? The evil one again? I stood still for a while. It seemed to move. Then I decided it was not moving. If I backed away, it would follow. I put out my hand—walked slowly toward it. I touched a black bear pelt. My legs collapsed under me. I cowered on the ground expecting the swipe of its claw. There was nothing. I could not stop shaking. Still it did not swipe. I reached my hand toward it. It was solid—not moving. A tree stump? I felt the moss I had thought was the bear's fur. I was ashamed of the fear I had felt. Surely I needed to be punished for my lack of faith.

I continued to gather wood for the fire.

For two months I traveled with the three men in the slapping wind. Two hundred miles. It was the way my mother had traveled as a captive—only she moved toward the Mohawk River and I was going away from it. The Jesuits had followed a map I could not read. I had felt it with my fingers in the mission. It was parchment. They moved my fingers along the trail they followed. I felt the parchment with my fingers. It felt pitted. I remembered it with my fingers. But these men traveled with the map in their heads.

I looked into the dark over us. The stars were brilliant, they said. I saw them as fuzz. But once in the night, coming awake for some reason, when I opened my eyes, I saw clearly for an instant—For one instant, I saw the clumps of stars like squirrels' nests in the sky—For one moment, I had clarity. The stars balled in the branches of the constellations. I saw these moments of clear vision. I felt it when I heard scriptures read. That was when my vision was clear. I saw the full moon clearly too. It was pock marked! Maybe smallpox had fallen from the moon. Or it had traveled there from here.

These little secrets of sight.

What field of corn: sight! What herd of deer in a time of hunger. I cried bitterly for the moment of clear sight as it passed from me.

We rode on the shoulders of the day. We moved from waterway across the land to waterway again. We crossed a large lake. We followed Indian trade routes. The paths of voyageurs and trappers. Animal trails. Our bed was the forest floor. The men set a few boughs on fire for warmth at night—and a watch-fire in the woods. There were voices in the ground. They spoke with tongues of dust and wind. I heard thunder and storm under the animal skin. I heard the animal's thoughts. Then the spirit of sleep came and wiped away the storm in the undergrowth of sleep.

What was this that drew me northward with it? I could not understand at first what I saw. My thoughts were a trickster. I could think this world was all there was, but the Jesuits said this world was a shadow. A crow's wing. We knew it anyway because of the Mohawk spirits. They came from a world other than this one. But the Jesuits said it was a world that burned with flames.

The hell they saved us from was a crow.

I saw the forest dreams. The little brown ribbons of snakes. The evil one who held my people in bondage. Who made us fight one another.

I remember the woman who had been scalped by the Machicans. I remember how we sat with her until she died.

Why do you want the day of the Lord? It is darkness, not light; as if someone fled from a lion and was met by a bear—Amos 5:19.

Father, we regret what we do.

Heartily.

Still we traveled. I felt the spots of sun and shade on the forest floor as we moved. The spots seemed as stars in the sky.

I heard old voices in the trees. Do we come back as trees? No, that is not so.

The hills surrounded us with their hands. I saw a flowering tree as if snow still on it. Then—what is this? The hills disappeared. What happened to them? Where did they go? The land was hills. Now there were none. Had the Maker flattened them with his foot when he stepped north to the new Caughnawaga? I felt afraid. Where had we come? This flat plain. This moraine? I did not like it.

Anastasia and Enit were there when I arrived. Also Fathers Fremin and Pierron from St. Peter's Mission. Fathers Chauchetiere and Cholenec had come from France.

I had to lie on my mat again. I saw wisps and swirls of air. I watched them with my eyes that could not see. I was seeing beyond seeing—I think it was the passing of wheels— the passing of cherubim wheels. I was with my *sisters*, Enit and Anastasia, again. The sky sat right down upon us.

Who are those across the river? I asked one afternoon when I was able to walk.

Trees, Enit answered.

They look like people raising their arms to our God, I said.

Yes, I would put the new land together with what I remembered of the old.

There were times I knew the trees had wings.

FATHER CLAUDE CHAUCHETIERE: St. Francis Xavier Mission, Caughnawaga, Sault St. Louis—We see from our way. Mightily. The Indians have their own beliefs. We cannot see from theirs. But it has to be our way, advanced as we are. We bring God's mercy and truth. We bring the way, the light. We have brought it all to them.

I read St. Ignatius by the candlelight. *Death will take from you the future, as it took from you the past, with the rapidity of lightning. And this is the life of all; the Holy Spirit says it is like the track of a ship on the ocean, the flight of a bird through the air. . . .*

KATERI: My people did not want to believe. I would be reparation for the sins of my people. I took off my beads and eel-skin ribbons. I scourged myself—Whipping a small branch against my back. I could not hit hard enough, but with repetition, the bark began to scrape my flesh. Finally, the bites of pain. I flinched. I trembled with each lashing. I shivered. In the rhythm, there was a will to suffer. It became an offering. A desired offering. I wanted to suffer. I felt God's judgment on sin. I smelled the sharp smell of his shed blood. I stood, holding onto the trees. I walked into this new, cold river—the St. Lawrence. I waded until it covered my chest—until I could hardly stand in the current. The spasms in my body drove me out. My skin shivered as if someone was lifting my flesh from me. My blood became the water. My bones became the fish.

I returned to the lodge. I would not eat. I would not allow a blanket on my bed.

Interrogation of the crows:

Who do you think you are? The crow asked.

Kateri Tekakwitha, I answered. The blessed one-who-trips-where-she-is-walking.

If he is God, could he take these pock marks from my face?

I was ashamed of that thought. I scourged myself again. It only took a short time to break into the fresh skin. In scripture, childbirth was the punishment for the woman. Thorns and thistles of the field for the man. I would not have children so I poked myself with thorns. I wore a hair shirt and iron girdle. I fell in a faint and when I woke, I found myself wrapped in animal robes. Anastasia and Enit sat by my bed. No more, they said. I floated in the warm robes. I felt God's warmth restore my bones.

On Christmas Day, 1677, I received my first communion at St. Francis Xavier Mission. I felt the wafer on my tongue. I drank Christ's blood shed for me. I felt unworthy. Unworthy.

There were times the Jesuits' chants were like the roar of wind high in the trees of the forest I had known in my village. I went back in thought, but pulled myself forward again.

We bring our diseases, our sins, our greed to this God who burns away everything he is not. The Word calls us the way we should go. I listened to scripture. I thought about the words of Daniel that Father Chauchetiere read that morning. I went over them and over them until they seemed to live before my feeble eyes.

I watched until the thrones were in place, and the Ancient One took his seat, whose garment was white as snow, and the hair of his head like pure wool; his throne was like fiery flames, and his wheels were burning fire. A fiery stream issued from him. A thousand thousands served him, and ten thousand times ten thousand stood before him. The judgment was set, and the books were opened.

I saw one like a human being, coming with the clouds of heaven. And he came to the Ancient One and was presented before him. To him was given dominion and glory and kingship, that all people, nations, and languages should serve him. His dominion is an everlasting dominion that will not pass away—Daniel 7:9–10, 13–14.

Nothing mattered but this.

These words flew higher than crows.

How much like thrones were thorns.

How the earth trembled at the shaking of these words.

The crows have come again to deliver these words, though that might not have been their intention. But it was the purpose they served.

When I am sick, I feel their wings.

When I see the white snow in the woods in summer, is it part of the Maker?—the Old One's garment?

I went to the church to pray in the middle of the night when Anastasia, Enit, and the others slept. I would have prayed to Kisisok?e, the Algonquin sun woman, if it were not for God. I longed for warmth. I hit myself with branches. I uncovered myself. I felt rigid with cold. I remembered the sun on my head as I sat by the Mohawk River in the old Caughnawaga. Sometimes I thought I could hear the fish. I remembered the red eel-skin ribbons I loved in my hair. I remembered the beading. I loved to roll the beads in my fingers. I loved my thimbles. Could I place them in the pits of my skin and bead my face, covering my skin with beads to hide my ugliness?

O God, there are opposites in this world. There are opposites of opposites that make a composite of oppositions. How do you expect us to follow you when there is this clutter in the way?

Because I loved glass beads, had God beaded my face?—Because I loved thimbles. I think the idea for hills came from thimbles. I think God's throne must be lined with thimbles. I think the church bells I hear are thimbles. I hit myself for that foolishness.

I ate, but mostly I fasted. I carried a tree in my burden strap. I would lie on my mat without my blanket. I would feel the cold gnaw at me. I could not sleep when I was shivering. It kept me awake to pray. To remember scriptures the priests had read. The Holy One hovered over me. I wanted him to extend his wings over all my people—over all the people.

I kept a metal candle-mold in the snow. I put it in my mat at my feet at night.

I have been washed in snow.

Yes, it is the snow on this flat land—when the moon is full, it is like the day. I can see the river, the trees on the other side of the river. I can see when the moon lights up the snow.

I felt an enormous place. I prayed for the land. For the unknown distances. I think it is as large as the ocean the Fathers say they crossed.

FATHER PIERRON: St. Francis Xavier Mission, Kahnawake or Caughnawaga—they never agree on anything. Satan has been with me this night. I cannot bring myself to explain the details—I can only say that his claws have been in my flesh.

KATERI: These fever dreams. These Mohawk gods. Evil— Every one of them. We were gathering wood. I saw my mother's face. Often I saw the faces of people in the woods who had died of smallpox. It must have been my poor eyesight. Maybe it was the other world that lived close to us.

I was fanned by crow wings. I saw berries yellow as a crow's eye. I would lift my stick against them, but I knew the Mohawk warning against the killing of crows.

The old stories rode on Tekawerahkhwa—the gusts of wind. I still heard them. My father told me the Mohawk story of the woman who fell from the sky and landed on a turtle. She had a daughter who had two sons who competed with one another—who always were at war. It was the journey within us. My mother had told me Algonquin stories.

The two brothers—Malsum and Gluskap—the one always trying to kill the other.

Flagellation was the crow's feet clawing.

I belonged to darkness. Not evil, but the light of heaven I could not see was a holy darkness in which I lived and had my being.

God is watchful as a crow. He squawks.

The Mystery wrapped in blackness. Did he have small-pox too? And could not be seen? Is that why he would only show Moses his backside of the wilderness?

During a winter hunt, there was a rumor: I slept with a hunter. But the rumor was wrong.

I taught prayers to children. I helped the sick. The accusations were not true.

Once, a hunter in exhaustion laid down beside my mat. When his wife woke, she saw him asleep near my mat and accused me of sleeping with her husband.

Father Cholenec questioned me. I said I had not. He believed me. He admitted me into the society within the group regarded as spiritual and without blame.

They are used to separate rooms they call their cells, but we slept together in the longhouse. We were never alone. I see this aloneness I feel is an enormous place. I know there is nothing but God. This mat. This candle. This bowl. This pitcher. These few twigs for heat.

Sometimes they told me I should marry. Had Anastasia remarried?

A woman, Marie-Therese Tegaiaguenta, came to St. Francis Xavier Mission after the death of her husband. She sat with her head bowed and did not say anything. Anastasia, Enit and I tried to talk to her, but she remained silent. She had been baptized by Father Bruyas. That was all she said.

I was working with Marie-Therese, pulling low branches off the trees, feeling for dead trees and brush for fire wood, when a branch fell from a tree and hit my head. I entered the blackness I saw before me. I thought I had died and entered the next world.

Who are these that fly like a cloud? These flying birds that were not birds.

Who are these? Lions again—I remember them in dreams when I was a child.

I felt my claws.

FATHER CLAUDE CHAUCHETIERE: St. Francis Xavier Mission—I read my Journal of the Nightmare—4th June 1678—The pitiful crossing of the Atlantic to Sault St. Louis on a ship. My stomach turns again to think of it. I was sick as soon as we left port. I vomited over the rail while land was still in sight. I stayed in the berth, so weak I could hardly rise. I was thirsty. My legs were water. I could not sleep. If I dozed off, I dreamed of water. I thought I would die. I hoped I would die to ascend to heaven to drink of the steams. Why this suffering? I was stowed with misery. My stomach was a knot that would take nothing into it. It leaped and fell like a large fish from the ocean. The priests gathered around me to pray. Others were sick, but none as sick as I was. The nausea was relentless. They said I cried in my sleep. I moaned when I was awake. They did not know what to do. They kept praying. Someone was always with me. Somewhere in the darkness, I heard a priest saying the last rights. I did not know where I was, but I knew the lifting and falling had not ceased.

Water.

Water.

Water.

It evaporated from the face of the earth. But this undrinkable water, this counterfeit water surrounding us, added to the agony. This drought, this parched sickness. Cobwebs filled my mouth.

I thought of Jonah in the whale's belly. I was not fleeing Tarshish, but headed toward it. I was a Jesuit on my way to convert the Indians. The savages waited on the far continent.

My stomach was a porpoise that jumped from the water. My throat heaved. It swelled. It was the ocean itself. I remember a bare thread of life. A filament. I clung to it.

Sometimes during nausea, my mouth watered. I was dry, yet my mouth watered? I continued to heave, but nothing was there. Lord have mercy. Jesus have mercy.

They put a small wad of cloth dipped in water to my mouth. I tried to eat it, choking. They had to dig it from my mouth. My hands tied down. A stick propped in my teeth to hold them apart.

My breath came and went like the ocean waves.

Then I heard, THERE IS LAND!!

I crawled onto the ground and wept. Thus, my glorious arrival in the New World.

I lit my candle and read from Psalm 107. I wept, remembering the crossing—The wretchedness—The horror of the moving box perched upon the nothingness of water.

They that go down to the sea in ships, that cross great waters. They see the works of the Lord and the wonders in the deep. The Lord commands and raises the stormy wind, which lifts up the waves thereof. They mount up to the heaven, they go down into the depths: their soul is melted because of trouble. They reel and stagger like a drunken man, and are at their wit's end. Then they cry to the Lord in their trouble, and he brings them out of their distresses. He makes the storm a calm, so that the waves thereof are still. Then they are glad because the waves are quiet; so he brings them into their desired haven—Psalm 107:23–30.

This God leads us through suffering. Does he watch the suffering or does he look away? What is he thinking when we go down to the sea in ships?

Fish swam beside the ship. Were they our guides? Were they in league with the wind and the ocean currents to bring us here? Were we puppets? Pawns in the hand of the Lord? I thought it was my own desires that brought me here. The icebergs in the distance. The whale that surfaced to look at us. Had it not seen whaling ships? Had it not been taught to fear even the merchant ships? The birds came as we neared shore.

Scripture is my haven. In scripture there is surety.

Sometimes I felt I was still on ship while on the new continent—trying to convert the rowdy Indians—yet a few came.

KATERI: This is my turn to say. I am telling the story. The prince of glory—deliver us to your side. Often now, I feel the heat of heaven even in the cold, the burning cold.

With the priests, we went to Laprairie, a French settlement on the island of Montreal. I saw a cart and understood wheels. I understood the cherubim on wheels. I saw commerce. Often I walked in silence—Other times I had more words than I could handle.

THE HORSE-LEECH'S DAUGHTERS: The horse-leech has two daughters: Give. Give, they cry—Proverbs 30:15.

They are like their father. They know his thirst—those daughters of the horse-leech that attaches itself to the horse's mouth.

How can I say these things I see in the French settlement? What is this rising like a river? Carts and wagons of a different kind of people. Lines of soldiers. Men on horses. Men, women, and children in wagons. Their cows following. Their crops. Where will we go? They will drive us away. I see what the Indians are up against. They will take our land. We will drown in their waters. We will be plowed under. Give. Give, they cry. Just a little piece of land. Their intent is a flock of crows. We will be eaten by the crows. They follow their plows like tail feathers.

But they bring a Book. Open it. Read. The Lord will transform our lives. We will not perish⌊We have everlasting life. It is the reason for crows. That we might know the Maker. They we might speak with the Ancient One.⌋

Have we not already been killed by their diseases? There are more of them than leaves. They made the noise of a snake when they pass. Their boats come onto our rivers.

What else is this I see in my vision? Clouds of darkness over the land. The sun and moon turned off. The people at a loss. Unspeakable grief and suffering. Is that what we bring upon ourselves by blinding our eyes to God? Is this the darkness the new people bring? Is it hidden in their wagons? Is it under the tarp in their boats?

The horse-leech has a party. His daughters wear their beads and eye paint. They have to suck. What else is there for them to do?

FATHER CHOLENEC: St. Francis Xavier Mission—This enormous frustration—To bring a complicated message and not be able to speak their language—and they unable to understand ours. How to explain what we have come to explain in the simplest terms—and there were other dialects—languages within language—How could it be explained? *Combien de langues faut-il pour ne rien savoir?* What joke was this?—Babel. What purpose? Yes—we were separated into the lonelinesses of our own language—Not able to speak—How many tongues does it pass through to reach another? And what is left of it once it arrives? And how do I know it has arrived? Look at the blank looks. Look at the discouragement. Look at the opportunity lost to turn them in a likeness of us.

KATERI: One day, finally, MARIE-THERESE TEGA-IAGUENTA spoke—We were hunting near the Ottawa River when there was a snowfall. After we ate the elk my husband killed, we were hungry, but could not hunt any longer in the deep snow. We ate bark and a few plants and roots we found. We even ate pieces of our moccasins. My husband was sick. Two men went to hunt. One returned without anything, but he did not have the starved look the rest of us had when he returned. He told us the other man had died.

They wanted me to abandon my husband. I would not. He died soon after the others left. The blackrobe had not baptized him. I buried him and left with my nephew whom I had adopted.

I found the Indians who had left me. They looked at me with suspicion. I soon discovered they were talking about killing someone to eat. It was an old man who could not keep up with them. He was going to die anyway. I could not eat his flesh. They looked at me with suspicion again. I wondered if they thought to kill me and the boy. We traveled toward a French settlement. A woman and her two boys were the next to be killed.

I carried my nephew on my shoulders. I knew we were next.

Suddenly there were animal tracks. We came upon a wolf, which we killed, and all of us ate.

I saw my nephew was blue. I rubbed his arms and legs. I forced a small plant in his mouth with a piece of the wolf meat.

I carried him the next day, but felt how light he was.

That night I buried him.

Enit, Anastasia, and I held our blankets around Marie-Therese as she talked. I have seen men force women to drink liquor, she said. I have seen things you have not. I have done things you have not.

We will do penance together, I told Marie-Therese. That way you can forgive yourself.

FATHER CLAUDE CHAUCHETIERE: When I saw the fever, the vomiting, the pain, and malaise of smallpox, I thought of the sickness I suffered on the ship. Would the memory of it stay with me to my own death?

The Jesuits of New France. I thought of the time when the continent would be French. The Dutch, English, Spanish, Portuguese would be gone. The Indians converted.

This never-complaining woman who already is praying in the church when I come in at 4:00 A.M. This *sauvagesse*. I guarded her though I knew she would not return to the shamans as other Indians did.

Is that a light I observe near her when she flagellates? A corposant? There was a ball of light at the top of the ship's mast during a storm. Was it not reported during the cross-ing of the Atlantic? But I was too weak to rise and see it.

When Father Pierron wrote me about her, he said she would never watch anyone being tortured, but she tortures herself? She knows how to do it. She must have watched.

It is hard to be a priest. How could I tell anyone what it is like? I am not worthy of my calling. I see them turn back to their old ways just when I thought the Indians were mine. Could I write letters of how many souls I have saved?

I came to help the Indians. Yet they would not receive my help—except a mute, pock-marked girl. Nothing I could do would change their suffering, their wars, their dis-eases, their deaths. My heart was black as a crow. I was suf-fused with hardship, disappointment, doubt. It was not working. I could not go back. I was to smooth the way for colonization when the Indians would be rid of their sav-agery. I heard of the torture and murder of Jesuits in the New World. I was not persuaded to worry. What I could not stand was the ineffectuality of my ministry. The Indians would not be persuaded. Yet the establishment of the Church for them in New France was my mission.

I was prepared to be a Jesuit martyr. I was prepared to face the barbarians. I was not prepared for indifference. For failure.

Was God asleep? I informed him of the problem in prayer.

Did not the cherubim carry our prayers in a bowl? Did they not sing a new song—you are worthy to take book and to open its seals for you were slain and have redeemed us to God by your blood? Revelation 5:8–9.

I see Katherine Tekakwitha tremble in prayer. I see her sickness. Often she stays on her mat in the longhouse. Smallpox is a ship that never reaches the other shore. Sometimes I feel prayer is also.

In this suffering, I think of your suffering on the cross.

I long sometimes to return to France—but a ship would be there.

KATERI: I picked wild cherries with Anastasia and Marie-Therese.

I still had dreams of spiders creeping over leaves. If I wanted to swat them, they would fly.

Do you not feel like a stranger in the world when you come back from disease?

The men fished for whitefish on the lake at night on the St. Lawrence. Once in a while, I sat in the canoe with Enit and her husband, Onas, and held the torch. Did the light not draw the fish to the surface where they could be speared by Onas and the others?

I watched the light reflected on the ripples of the lake. How they were a fuzz of stars in heaven. How often, I felt the hook from another world.

In the summers, we ate wild fish packed with cherries.

We prayed and watched the heavens twist.

This God is not made up by the church. This is real.

CAW!!! CAW!!! FATHER CLAUDE CHAUCHETIERE: I must remind myself, I admire their politics. The Mohawk, Oneida, Onondaga, Cayuga, and Seneca had become the Five Iroquois League of Nations under a leader named Deganawidah. Yet I see the terrible raids of these people on one another—Infants roasted while their mothers watched in hysterical fits of grief followed by rage. Have you seen a savage enraged? Others burn the soles of the enemies' feet and thighs with firebrands. No, I cannot admire their ways. I flagellate myself to make correction of the course I follow. How terrible their ways—

The Indians steal other Indians to replenish what they had lost. It was how Katherine Tekakwitha's mother had become a Mohawk. The Indians stole people from other tribes. Brutalized them, then integrated them into their tribe to replace the lost.

I think this disease of smallpox is God's punishment upon the Indians because they refused him.

I hear them speak of dreams. Certain dreams mark passage into an adult. What dreams did Katherine Tekakwitha have? I asked her. She dreamed of the French invading. She dreamed of the Machicans invading. She dreamed of smallpox invading. She dreamed of spiders. She dreamed they had wings. She could not walk without stepping on them. She dreamed of people everywhere, crowding out the forest. That is enough of your dreaming, I said.

FATHER _____: This bruised world MANGLED by the will. I have become a burden. A weight. A dejected lump. I am a shame to the priesthood. I am weak. I cannot climb above this rock.

KATERI: I dreamed I had claws and a wing made of a mat of dried moss.

FATHER CHOLENEC: St. Francis Xavier Mission—I lost my parents as a youth. As did St. Ignatius. If only I could write like him. I wonder if I would be a priest if my parents had lived. The death of a parent is a ship's crossing. But there was famine and squalor in France also during Louis XIV. I thought of the working of Providence. I came to the Jesuits as an orphan. I felt the working of God as an orphan. It had been a blessing. I cannot explain it. Where did that feeling go?—A well-being in the midst of dire circumstances.

FATHER CLAUDE CHAUCHETIERE: In the night, I heard one of the priests coughing. It was an endless cough-ing—A coughing from the pit of his belly, or was it some-where within his spirit?—as if trying to dislodge something that had caught there. I pushed back the animal skins the Indians gave us and got up from my bed and crossed the floor to the priest. My feet were frigid. I was walking on ice, stepping across the frozen waves. I could walk and not sink. It was steady. Not rocking up and down, upsetting my very soul. Yet I was dislodged by the crossing.

FATHER CHOLENEC: I put my hands upon the priest's head and prayed with Father Chauchetiere. Magnificent Lord, you carry healing in your wings. You can do all things. Relieve my brother from his affliction. Remove the thorn from his flesh. I think of the depth of our sin and depravity. It was myself I was praying for. My own disruptions.

I felt the unsteadiness of my childhood. This is what it felt like to have no parents. This is what it was to be without the Lord.

FATHER CHAUCHETIERE: Will he never stop coughing?—This priest at war with himself. Finally, his coughing lessened. Or I grew used to it and was able to sleep. Not as disrupted. Circumvented. Gone around. Was it possible to travel to a far place by land? Did it always include a passage by water? Namely the sea. I thought of the valley of bones. Sinew and flesh upon this bones. I shall live and you shall live, and we shall know that you are the Lord of hosts.

Katherine Tekakwitha thinks Ezekiel is the only book in the Bible. Father de Lamberville hit that book too hard. He read her too much. I will have to write to him. We have to keep it from them. We have to nurture. Direct. It should come from us. We are the go-between between parishioners and Christ. What if they knew they could approach God on their own? With only the blood of Christ between. What would it do for us? How fragile. How insignificant. What are these strips of rebellion I feel within me? I desire to be rid of them. Cough them up. Dispel them.

It burns so intensely, it cannot last long.

These women. These hosts of deception. We must remember their frailty. We must see them as your subjects, O God. They seem to understand somewhat. Some of them.

We are bothered by these Indians. Their ways have a hold on them. They are against your ways, O God. We come to instruct. To show them the way. But they will not have us. They have killed priests. They do not seem to understand we bring the message of the Holy God. Strike them with thunderbolts this spring. Get rid of this cold. Turn the winter over and make spring come out on top.

I remember a boy's game. Cornering a boy—beating him until he came to school the next day with a black eye. Ostracizing him. Maybe his father had beaten him too because he let himself be picked on. Forgive me, Jesus. I confess my meanness. My harshness. Is there any doubt of our evil? It is why you hang on the cross. Give me respite from my guilt, O Lord. Give me respite from this cold at St. Francis Xavier Mission. My place to gather souls to you. They will not come, most of them. What is wrong with them? I explain your kingdom and some of them come for a while, then walk back to their heathen ways. Heathens all of them. Let hell fires burn them. Let their tongues hang out. Let them be parched. Let them know the disappointment I feel over them. Gang up on them with your priests, your cherubim. Your chariots. Let me go after them with a stick. No, revenge belongs to the Lord—Rope them in. Get them. Get them. Scourge them with your rod of iron. I hold them open to you.

I hear confession, but they do not know what to say. They are not aware of their sins. What do they think of this crucifixion? This hanging upon thorns. This hanging on thrones.

I need a handkerchief for my running nose.

A shy blue haze was in the room. Barely. Dawn. Another day.

For some reason, I hold the memory of my boyhood room. A blue bowl on a table. A bed.

This harshness. Harshness. My bones hurt. My breath in the frozen air. We wore our cloaks to bed for warmth. Is it not now summer?? The fields are blooming in France— but I have this flowering of my breath in the cold!!

This suffering—this life. This sore encrusted on my nose. This congestion. I am heartily sorry for my discomfort. For my complaints. I accept this assignment. This outpost. This mortification of my flesh. Use it as a prod to drive me to you. Not my will, O Lord, but Yours. This unending coldness. My hurt. My sore muscles. My eyes burn. Help me to spurn this discomfort. To say to an evil spirit, who are you? I do not know you. I belong to the Lord of Hosts. The Lord of the Cherubim. They are favorites of Katherine Tekakwitha. She likes their wheels. In the French settlement, Laprairie, I stopped a cart so she could feel the wheels. They were muddy. She was covered with it, but she understood the wheels she loves. She could see somewhat— she knew the ground was marked with cart wheels going different ways. She could feel the grooves, or knew they were there. Yes, she knew wheels, she said. Somehow that thrilled her.

I come before You, O Lord, with my reserve. My trouble with wandering in my prayers. My fortification in horror. My ocean crossing as haunting as if it were still in progress. I come to You as a boy who has lost his parents. You are my Refuge. My Fortress. Underneath are Your Everlasting Arms.

We have so much to encourage us. St. Ignatius. St. Xavier. St. Theresa.

This meditation is from St. Ignatius.

Enter into the heart of Jesus Christ. Prayer is constantly united in it to the work of the hands. In the midst of bodily fatigues, Jesus blesses the justice of His Father that has condemned man to water the earth which gives him bread with the sweat of his brow—Genesis 3:19.

Today, I feel less fragile, less violent, more discerning. Let them walk on their little crab feet. Let them go sideways. Let them be sucked out of their shells. Let them squawk like hens going to the chopping stump. I am feeling I have a handle on the priesthood. I should not think so much of hell. Give me a gentler spirit. Let me be content with the water of my condemnation.

Most merciful God, I beseech You. Give us Emanations against this Privation. These Illnesses. These Corrections pulling me to themselves. This Solitude. This Companion. This coughing priest. Not the Living Immaculate God, but this diminished idea I have of You. Heal me, Lord, let me see the Correction of Your Light. This poverty frightens me. This lack of strength of my own. Nothing stands against the knowledge of the day that pulls us from this life. Once we were in Eden, but we sinned. God had to send us away fast. Before we became a living power he could not let go of that would burn his hand.

I think we are all tossed from the tumbler. Most will make it. Some will make it. Did it work by plan? Or was it happenstance. Who would get sick on the ship. Who would not. Who would die with smallpox. Who would live.

Father de Lamberville asks about Kateri. I think it is good they are apart.

KATERI: I loved beading. Now I bead with prayers. At the St. Francis Xavier Mission, I teach the girls.

This is how to pound corn. . . . This is how to tell a story. . . . This is the likeness of both. This is how to make a wampum belt for conducting the affairs of the Iroquois nation. We will send them to St. Peter's Mission at Caughnawaga for dispersement. I received a letter from Father de

Lamberville in return—He is well. He exhorts me to take care of myself.

I hear the traffic on the river. The traders come for deer skins and beaver pelts. They stand in the air pestered with insects. I hear them swat at them. The priests call the deer, *wild cows*. They see the world in their own way.

In return for our beading and hides, the priests receive hatchets, knives, kettles, salt, sulfur, powder, lead, porcelain beads, blankets. They give the beads to the Indians they are trying to convert.

When the traders leave, we have kettles hanging over the fire. I work with Anastasia, Enit, Marie-Therese, and the other women to make Indian bread. We have corn boiled in water. The men bring pigeons. Others bring fish. The women find grapes, plums, and berries. It is the *commerce* we learn.

I still bead moccasins and deerskin shirts. I still dye threads and porcupine quills. I make head pieces for the men, banded with a beaded wampum belt, covered with pheasant feathers and a plume. Sometimes I work with shells, but mostly beads.

I take part in the ceremonial planting. I sing the song of the digging sticks. We scrape together small mounds of soil and plant seeds of corn, beans, squash. We wrap them in prayer. The trail of smoke from burning tobacco takes our words to God. I do not see how he could be displeased with the smoke. I do not agree with the priests. Is it not the same as their censer?

Weeding was time for more prayers. Also harvesting, drying, storing. We had feasts of thanksgiving. The priests tolerated some of our old ways.

What did I want? To live the vision I had received. To keep my commitment to Christ. To flee the wolves of the flesh. I saw the glory of God, and it was all that mattered. I saw the hellfires and wanted to do penance for my people. I burned myself with firebrands. I touched them to my legs. I felt the burnings through the night, long after the firebrands had gone out. That was the way it was with torture. I had heard the Machicans wail after the torturing stopped. The pain lasted beyond the torturing. It kept torturing. That was the horror of torture. They also knew they would be tortured the next day and the next—They knew they would be tortured slowly to death. It would not stop. I burned myself to understand more of hell—of the torture of hell—so I could tell my people what it was like. So I would know the burning and its throbbing aftermath. So I would know how to pray. To make the Indians understand because I understood there is a heaven, and underneath it, there is a hell.

We are refugees from the incoming ones. We are captives to our darkness unless we have the light of Christ. Even then there is suffering—

I hear the priest read the sufferings of the believers in the New Testament. The Apostle Paul is as bitten as the priests. Maybe they caught it from him.

I am bitten too. I wake in the night. Or is it sleep? I am turning over in the clouds. I hear a voice. It is Marie-Therese.

She is beside me. She is holding me to the earth. I am praising God. I try to get loose, but she will not let go.

FATHER CLAUDE CHAUCHETIERE: I first heard of the New World at St. Parchaire parish school near Portiers—It was a land across the sea. I knew a priest had been martyred there.

What was I doing here? Why the priesthood? Because they took me in when I was orphaned. They gave me purpose.

When Katherine Tekakwitha was sick, it was *Jesus Blessed Savior* I heard. She was not one of the fickle Indians who returned to their dreams. Her transformation was complete.

There was a new vigor of the church when she came to the St. Francis Xavier Mission. There was a putting away of past failures. She was one of the leaders.

She listened as I read the words of the Apostle Paul—

They were stoned, they were sawn asunder, were tested, were slain with the sword; they wandered in sheepskins and goatskins; being destitute, afflicted, tormented (of whom the world was not worthy); they wandered in deserts, and in mountains, and in dens and caves of the earth— Hebrews 11:37–38.

There is snowfall before me. There is a snowwall. I can break through not by direct approach, but by several attacks, random, not related, but someone all working together. Not organized, but poked at, stabs here, stabs there, not hitting directly, but making random, unrelated stabs looking back over what I had written, hoping later I would see the trail, yes, I could do it afterward.

The sacraments and priest duties. The Eucharist. The very wine and wafer itself became the blood and flesh of Christ.

My ribs ache from the coughing I caught from him. I felt the transmogrification of the priesthood. Its emissives.

I felt the complaints of the Old Testament prophets to God about the rebellious people.

Did he send the Indian girl as an encoded message? I had to watch God. He had become tricky.

We spend all day in prayer. In the night, I hear my dreams pray.

KATERI: Blue strips of bark hang from the sky. When I stand in the river, the wind is a blue smoke. My trusty rider, the fire. I feel it in the stripes on my bones. Christ appears wrapped in animal skins. Deer hooves for his feet. An antler on his head. He has four faces. I feel his stripes. I see the four faces revealed in suffering. The stripes. The scorchings. The scourgings. The freezings. I sleep while awake. The crows cackle. Their stark wings flutter over me like a priest's stiff frock. They are noisy, noisy—Would someone tell them to be quiet? I could not sleep but was pulled upon their wings. I feel my arms in their beaks to pull me up from this earth. I do not know where I am. Strangely, I am not afraid. I rejoice in the air though they could drop me any moment. I feel a lightness in my head. I feel like I could slip out of this world.

FATHER CLAUDE CHAUCHETIERE: What about Ezekiel fascinated Father de Lamberville? It is a rough book with sharp transitions. Ezekiel knew deportation. He was one of the Jewish exiles taken to Babylon. He was completely devoted to his religion.

I rose from the table and walked in the room. This hard floor. This hard table. This hard truth. It lit my imagination. No wonder the priests coughed.

Why did God's kingdom have so much suffering attached to it?

In journeyings often, in perils of waters, in perils of robbers, in perils by my own countrymen, in perils by the heathen, in perils in the city, in perils in the wilderness, in perils in the sea—2 Corinthians 11:26.

How often the apostle Paul spoke of his torments. Being reviled, we bless; being persecuted, we endure it—1 Corinthians 4:12.

These words are ice. I slip on them. I am afraid.

These encrypted messages. These inscriptions from my imaginations.

Even unto this present hour we hunger, and thirst, and are naked, and are buffeted, and have no certain dwelling place—1 Corinthians: 4:11.

In stripes, in imprisonments, in tumults, in labors, in watchings, in fastings—2 Corinthians 6:5.

I was beaten with rods, once I was stoned, THREE TIMES I SUFFERED SHIPWRECK, A NIGHT AND A DAY I HAVE BEEN IN THE DEEP, in journeyings often,

IN PERILS OF WATER, in perils of robbers, in perils by my own countrymen, in perils by the heathen, in perils in the city, in perils in the wilderness, IN PERILS IN THE SEA, in weariness and painfulness, in watchings often, in hunger and thirst, in fastings often, in cold and nakedness—2 Corinthians 11:25–27.

St. Ignatius of Loyola, of the Society of Jesus, had been a soldier. He understood these scriptures. In withstanding the French, his leg was shattered, and when it did not heal, was reset in a manner he called butchery. Sometimes he went in solitude into the caves. By fasting and confession, his vigor returned.

FATHER CHOLENEC: I saw Kateri pass before the window as I worked on our journals, which are required. I was horrified!! There almost was nothing left of her—What are you doing, child?

KATERI: I felt the crow wing over me. I do not know what world I was in. I hardly felt the transition—except it was easy to move—to walk—to see. I was somewhat dazed. There was a place far ahead of me—I was not there yet. This unction. This unction has become my choice word. I heard his voice, Go between the wheels under the cherub, Fill your hands with coals of fire and scatter them over the land, Over your people. The longhouse was filled with the cloud and in the cloud was the Brightness of the Lord. I heard the sound of the cherubim's wings. It was the high roar of wind in the forest. Stand between the wheels, and they lifted me—I rose among the trees as a tree I was lifted to the sky. I was not through spreading the coals—wait—wait! I am not finished—I want penance for my father, my uncle Iowerano, and the Indians who do not believe—But they were around me on all four sides. I rode with the cherubim, Over us was the throne and on the throne the Glory of God—Ezekiel 10. Yet I lived and was not dead.

This morning the Lord spoke to me: *I could have flown from the cross, but I waited for you.*

FATHER CLAUDE CHAUCHETIERE: St. Francis Xavier Mission—Sometimes I grew a little melancholic—when I see these heathens, these Indian families, when I see how they live as one. My father died when I was sixteen. He was a lawyer—he wore a black robe too. We were an established family. Then he was gone and I knew poverty. I was alone. I took my initial vows. I was eighteen. What did I know? At the age of twenty-three I was transported in the Spirit to the Spirit. I knew I would be a priest. In 1678 I moved to the pagan world across the sea. It had taken nearly ten years to become a Jesuit. Yet in this world, the years felt no more than a strip of seaweed.

KATERI: There are more horrors. I know them though I cannot see the details. An assembly was held for new converts who came to the mission. They were battered with their hardships. Some of them had tears. One had a severe wound. The Jesuits applied a plaster and prayed, but he died the next day. Some left the mission. A few stayed. Someone stole a moose skin. The priests blamed the Huron. Or the Iroquois. They knew they came to the village at night. But there were others. Why did they not blame the Dutch or French? There were terrible tortures. Some arrived at the mission having had boiling water poured into their wounds, mocking the holy baptism. Other victims told of seeing strips of burned flesh cut from the captives, then eaten before them. What must hell be like if this is what happens on earth? Sometimes the priests could not look at us in their horror of the savages.

I felt a swoon—a going away of myself. I grow closer to my Lord in heaven everyday. Sometimes I shiver as if standing in the cold water.

Now it is someone with a snake bite, swollen and black. There are ulcers and open sores. Now it is someone with convulsions. Not smallpox, but something else.

FATHER CLAUDE CHAUCHETIERE: St. Francis Xavier Mission—I see Katherine Tekakwitha stumble away from helping the wounded. I know she will die. But I thought she would die before. I see her sick and frail body. She is so small and thin. How did life stay in her? I hear her vomit. I see the paroxysms of her body as it wretches long after there is nothing to bring up.

KATERI: This day I see the lion again—I see him as I did long ago. I see him with a mane of light around his head!!! It envelops me also.

FATHER CLAUDE CHAUCHETIERE: I felt her fever. She held her stomach and curled up on her mat. She was not much more than a sapling. She was near death many times. She almost longed for it.

KATERI: He returns as a lion!! I feel his jaws on my arm. I feel him take me—A lion with wings??—That flies taking others with him??

Do I hear him on the cross—Or is it the nailing of the rain on the bark of the longhouse?

Is this marriage to Christ? The going away with him—the longing to stay with him—the belonging nowhere else. It is his border I desire.

FATHER CHOLENEC: I heard the women's cries. What was it? *Elle se meurt.* Someone was running. Oh, it is Kateri. She is dead. No!! *Elle est morte!!*

FATHER CLAUDE CHAUCHETIERE: St. Francis Xavier Mission—When she died, I was afraid of her. She went willingly. It was as if she lapped at the water from the holy streams. Her tongue made strange motions. Her fingers curled as if claws.

We watched death come over her. It sat on her like a bird. We felt a strange breeze, though we saw nothing. On

Wednesday, 17th April 1680, at the age of twenty-four, she died at 3:00 in the afternoon.

Jesos Konoronkwa, she said, Jesus, I love you.

I swear I heard a distant roar. I even looked toward the woods.

The Jesuits and all the Indians crowded in the small room. We saw the scars on her face disappear. Her fingers uncurled. Her skin was smooth in death.

KATERI: Why would we be born in this body? To mortify it as it mortifies us. Until I hold the world like a berry in my hand. Why are some drawn to this? Why do others give it away? Just because they cannot see? Just because they choose not to believe? And why did I? Because I had nothing else? Because I was pitiful? Sometimes children ran from me. When I had walked in the French settlement, I knew people stared. I could not see them clearly, but I could feel their eyes. I did not want to go again. If a boat stopped on the St. Lawrence, I knew the people turned their eyes. I was dust. I was one of those who had survived the smallpox. I was nothing but a curiosity to them. Would I have run to God if I was not pocked? Yes, I would. I believed. Why? I had an assurance that God was. Though with sorrow I knew my people—the Mohawk—the Algonquin—the Indians did not. They wanted to stay with their own gods.

Despise the words of those who have no faith—That is what I said as I left. I was floating in the river. A Spirit lowered its basket. I was in the water that spilled into the

Spirit's basket. I was lifted. I was taken to heaven. The passage was much like my travel from St. Peter's to the St. Francis Xavier Mission. There were others with me. My mother, father, and brother. I tried to see them but I could not. I wondered if the others were Hot Ashes, Enit's husband, Onas, and Jacque, the other man I had traveled with, but I knew they were not. Still, I wanted to ask who they were, but I was not to think of them, but of the passage. Were they guides? Were they guards? Were they traveling like me? There was darkness swimming over us. It was full of terrible beings. I had to keep my mind on the way ahead. The beings would pull me. They would taunt. Was I an enemy in their camp? Were they there to torture? Yes, they would if they could. But there was something keeping them from me. Yet they could hit. They could hiss. They could scare. But there was something stronger than them. I had felt it on my travel from St. Peter's Mission. Over us there is something great and terrible and sweeping—against which everything else is powerless.

Jesus Christ it is only you.

FATHER CLAUDE CHAUCHETIERE: St. Francis Xavier Mission—There was excessive penance of other Indians after Kateri died. On Good Friday, the sermon on the Passion of Christ was interrupted by the lamentation of the parishioners. All they could talk about was the transformation of her appearance. This mix of Indian grieving and Christian remorse at her loss.

I waited for the apparitions. I was not disappointed. I saw her as I prayed at her grave. I saw her with the crucifix in her hand. I saw a church turned on its side.

FATHER CHOLENEC: *My pious savage—*

FATHER CLAUDE CHAUCHETIERE: Father Pierre Cholenec cried. I rarely saw him moved.

FATHER CHOLENEC: *Deus Dominus, et illuxit nobis.* It is God who is the author of this great light.

FATHER PIERRON: St. Francis Xavier Mission—Kahnawake or Caughnawaga—Sault St. Louis—south bank of St. Lawrence River—west of the Atlantic Ocean—Montreal—The New World—Whatever World—I cannot bring myself to tell all the details, but this I will say—No, I do not know how to write what I want to say. I will keep the particulars to myself.

KATERI: The World Above—There is no smallpox there. That is the first thing I can say. Though I looked for it.

I do not know what the Jesuits were thinking. I do not think they knew what they were thinking. But they were close to heaven in what they said. Or in what the scriptures said.

I look back at the earth. There are crow wings of darkness over it. But in places the light of the Lord God is broken into brilliant flashes of light that do not hurt my eyes.

I can see! I can walk without tripping.

After death I went to the longhouses. I stood by the sleeping mats of Enit, Marie-Therese Tegaiaguenta, and Anastasia Tegonhatsiongo with my cross that grew hot in my hand as it shined nearly blinding the women when they looked at it. When I heard them say my name, I left.

The Indians believe that the dead linger near their bodies for a few days after death. It was because they were looking for me that they saw. My place is no longer with them.

There are cherubim in heaven as Father James de Lamberville told us there were. Rolling on their wheels. I will visit with Ezekiel. His house is there over that hill.

These are the wheels of voices from the Book. They are louder now than the voices of the trees.

FATHER JAMES DE LAMBERVILLE: St. Peter's Mission, Caughnawaga—Sometimes at night, she returns to me uncut.

KATERI: I saw a flock of black crows. What fire had they passed through on their way from earth? What was over the earth that burned what passed through it? Were the crows' cherubim who had gone to earth, who had endured the fire to come to us? Was the purpose of the crows to turn us toward the cherubim? This darkness. This darkness. These crows. These crows. They were smallpox. They were our burned fields. They were my heart. They were the Jesuits who brought the knowledge of hell—who told us, above this world of disease, and the pit of hell beyond it, was the hope of heaven. In this darkness so dark sometimes that even God seemed dark—was the light that dispelled the darkness. The light only seemed wrapped in darkness—but the darkness was its carrier—its shell. The light that overcame the darkness was inside.

Heaven was much like it was in the scriptures of the Book.

FATHER JAMES DE LAMBERVILLE: St. Peter's Mission—after the Death of K. T.—I opened my Bible to Ezekiel. I looked and a wind came out of the north: a great cloud with brightness around it and fire flashing forth continually. In the middle of it was something like four living creatures. They each had four faces and four wings. Their feet were like a calf's hoof, and they sparkled like burnished bronze. Under their wings they had human hands. The four had faces of a human being, a lion, an ox, and an eagle. Each moved straight ahead, wherever the spirit would go, they went, without turning they went.

In the middle of the living creatures there was something that looked like burning coals of fire, like torches moving through the woods where we walked or when we *fire-fished* in the Mohawk River. The fire was bright, and lightning came from the fire. The living creatures moved like flashes of lightning.

As I looked at the living creatures, I saw a wheel on the earth beside the living creatures, one for each of them.

When they moved, they moved in any of the four directions without veering as they moved.

Their rims were full of eyes. Wherever the spirit would go, they went, and the wheels rose along with them; the spirit of the living creatures was in the wheels. When they moved, the others moved; when they stopped, the others stopped; and when they rose from the earth, the wheels rose with them.

Over the heads of the living creatures there was something like a firmament, spread out above their heads. Under the firmament their wings were stretched out straight, one toward another. When they moved I heard the sound of mighty waters, like the thunder of the Almighty, a sound of tumult like the sound of an army; when they stopped, they let down their wings.

Above the firmament over their heads there was something like a throne. And seated above the likeness of the throne was something that seemed like a human form. This was the appearance of the likeness of the glory of the Lord—from Ezekiel 1:4–28.

KATERI: Above the World—There was an opening of light. I saw the cherubim that bore the weight of the throne, with four faces, wings, hoofed feet, and wheels. They reflected the light of God that came from the opening. I saw the cherubim had faces of a man, a lion, an ox, and eagle. Once again, I fell on my knees—this time it was because of the glory I saw.

What can I say of them?—Whoso bears God's praises, bears his likeness.

Then I looked above the cherubim—and saw on the throne the glory that was God.

CHERUBIM: Holy. Holy. Holy.

AFTERWORD

Historical fiction: isn't the term itself an oxymoron?
— *Truth or Whoppers: On Writing
Historical Fiction,* Valerie Martin

IT WAS JUST BEFORE Christmas, December 20, 2005, that the first lines for this book came to me: *The moaning was my first memory. I think it was them—my mother and father.* I looked up information on Kateri Tekakwitha on the Internet. I got a book from the library, *Mohawk Saint* by Allan Greer. I got other books. On January 1, I went to my cabin in the Missouri Ozarks and continued writing and reading. I found the usual discrepancies of history. Tekakwitha's name was Ka teri. Her name was Kat er ee. Her name was Got ah lee. She was four or six when her parents died. Certain information disagreed. But the story was there: a Mohawk girl suffered smallpox as a child. She was converted to the faith the Jesuits brought. She died at age twenty-four. She appears on the lower left panel of the front doors of St. Patrick's Cathedral in New York City as Ven. Kateri Tekakwitha. The smallpox scars are visible on her face. A print by

Father John B. Giuliani, *Blessed Kateri Tekakwitha*, appears on the cover of *Flutie*, another book of mine.

In May 2006, I drove from Kansas City to upstate New York and Montreal to visit Ossernon and both Caughnawagas. Seven hundred thirty-two miles the first day; five hundred thirty-two miles the second; and three hundred two miles the third. I stopped in Auriesville, N.Y., the site of Ossernon, the village where Kateri was born, on a hill above the Mohawk River. I visited the museum. Then I crossed the river at Fonda, N.Y., off U.S. I–90, where her people had moved to a new village, Caughnawaga, also on a hill, upstream, on the other side of the Mohawk. I visited another museum and walked up a hill where stakes outlined the site where the village had been. A sign pointed the way to the spring that had provided water for the village and Kateri's baptism. In the field I passed, I found a single cut lily lying on the ground. Later in the afternoon, I drove to Kahnawake on the south bank of the St. Lawrence River, Montreal.

While I traveled, I listened to books on tape. I took notes on the landscape of upstate New York—the rock outcroppings were nearly black, much darker than the limestone embankments in the Midwest. I thought about Kateri. I remembered once reading an essay about a woman who stopped for prayer, *keeping hours*. Even if she was driving, she pulled off the road. My prayer, on the contrary, happens in moving. I write while traveling—I took note of the hills and forest surrounding the Mohawk River. I took note of the level plain of Canada by the St. Lawrence River.

One of the essays I listened to on tape was John Muir's "Stickeen," about his 1880 exploration of southeastern Alaska, in what is now Taylor Bay. He wrote of crossing a high, narrow ice bridge over a crevasse with a dog, Stickeen. He called it a "razor" bridge. I tried to think of the immediacy of the crossing as I worked with Kateri's passage from her culture into Christianity.

In *The Writer's Chronicle*, February 2006, volume 38, number 4, Valerie Martin says, "History is, after all, really just another place." For me, a historical *place,* actually, is historical *places.* I see a historical space as a room with several perspectives. Mine is an austere Protestant approach.

The Catholic Church is in the process of canonizing Kateri Tekakwitha. I wanted to write a side of her story from a native perspective—not what others said about her—although I wanted her voice interspersed with voices of the priests. I also wanted to explore Christianity from a native understanding without the shrubbery of religion. I wanted to find the primitiveness that had been on the land—I felt it was where I would find Kateri's voice.

History takes place depending on who is speaking. (My daughter and I, for example, have different versions of the history we share.) The same *space* in history has different furniture, different portraitures on the wall, and rugs of various blends, patterns, designs, complexities, complications.

I like to explore a story lost in the past with various versions and various characters from various inconsistent perspectives. I see truth as a delivery of the one delivering—especially when it delivers what has been lost and there is no tracking number. I am not talking about the Lord's Truth—the Immutable Truth—The I-Am-That-I-Am. But historical truth that often varies—the individual histories out of the mainstream History. Truthful history—I like this necessary oxymoron. The history of truth is these incoherent versions—this residue of the past we are left with. There are many versions of the same event, and in some sense, all will be true if only to the one telling it.

In 2006, I visited the Dada exhibit at the National Gallery in Washington, D.C. Some of the work reminded me of a collage I had made of a claw and wing. "Everything had broken down . . . and new things had to be made out of fragments," Kurt Schwitters, a German assemblage artist, wrote. Brokenness certainly was the case for Kateri Tekakwitha, who saw the fracturing of herself, her family and tribe in a brutal time of hunger, disease, ongoing war with other tribes, the European migration into the land, and the arrival of the Jesuits who wanted to dig up the Mohawk spiritual beliefs and reset them with their own. The genre of historical writing itself is a collage work. It is an overlayering of nonfiction with fiction. I gathered found objects of information from museums, from books, from travel to the land where the history took place. Historical fiction is an upheaval. An assemblage of voices. A distortion. A making space for the surface of recording.

BIBLIOGRAPHY

Bechard, S. J., Henri. *Kaia'tano:Ron Kateri Tekakwitha.* Trans. Antoinette Kinlough. Kahnawake, Quebec: Kateri Center, 1994.

Buehrle, Marie Cecilia. *Kateri of the Mohawks.* Milwaukee, Wisc.: Bruce Publishing, 1954.

Bunson, Margaret. *Kateri Tekakwitha, Mystic of the Wilderness.* Huntington, Ind.: Our Sunday Visitor, 1992.

Cholenec, S. J., Pierre. *Catherine Tekakwitha.* Trans. William Lone, S. J. Auriesville, N.Y.: Tekakwitha League, 2002. (Originally published in the 17th century.)

Cohen, Leonard. *Beautiful Losers.* New York: Bantam Book, 1967.

Greer, Allan. *Mohawk Saint.* New York: Oxford University Press, 2005.

Weiser, S. J., F. X. *Kateri Tekakwitha.* Montreal, Quebec: Kateri Center, 1971.